R.A.Watson-Wood

Disclaimer

This is a work of fiction. Names, characters, businesses, places, events, locales, and incidents are either the products of the author's imagination, or used in a fictitious manner. Any resemblance to actual persons, living or dead, or actual events is purely coincidental.

Unless, that is, I was completely and utterly inspired by a certain person, place, or thing. In which case any similarity may be considered a great honour.

Any resemblance to any person, place or thing described in this book in a bad light should be referred back to the first paragraph of this disclaimer, obviously.

R.A.Watson-Wood

ISBN: 9781980653929

Imprint: Independently published

DEDICATION

For Claire, who started me off
and Clara, who spurred me on

ACKNOWLEDGMENTS

To Richie, Laura, my children and the rest of my family. Thank you for putting up with me. My grateful thanks to my former colleagues, for providing inspiration, and great memories. To current colleagues and fellow creatives, thank you for the encouragement to continue and follow my dream

1

The siren of Sasha's alarm clock was the worst sound in the world. Especially considering the dream it had just intruded upon.

In a split second, the shock of being woken gave way to a most intense anger at the clock, followed by the miserable realization that what she'd just experienced was actually just dream.

Highly realistic, mind you – Sasha could feel her heart beating with passion and a very real tingling between her thighs , so much so that the first thing she could think of doing was to finish herself off in the shower. She threw back the covers and sighed, pursing her lips for a moment before throwing herself out of bed, and headed for the bathroom.

Sasha closed her eyes and washed away her disappointment and the warm water rinsed over her body. The realization that the man of her dreams was just that, a dream figure that existed only in that moment between sleep and awake, darkened her mood so much so that she could see the day ahead being a long and tedious one.

As with countless other nights before this one, she had been totally and utterly in love with this imaginary figure; and now had to face the reality that he didn't exist. It wasn't like he even had a real face, one that she could recall and describe in detail. She had made him up; or at least her subconscious had.

Drat. Back to real life; ex-boyfriends; workplace crushes; and the daily grind. Sasha took a deep breath and pouted at herself in the mirror as she smoothed down the pencil skirt of her uniform.

"Get a grip" she told her reflection out loud. She grabbed her uniform-issue handbag off the bed and left, slinging her work security pass over her head and round her neck as she went.

It was a cool, early autumn day as she walked to the train station; mild enough to not make her shiver and rush to get out of the cold. She was slightly ahead of herself and took her time, making the most of the time to herself to gather her thoughts, and breathe the fresh air deeply in an effort to clear her head.

"Aww come on Sash, it'll happen eventually." Sasha's best friend and work colleague, Leigh, comforted as she handed Sasha a takeaway coffee from the platform refreshment booth, "Mister Right has to be out there somewhere." Sasha took the cup from her friend and pursed her lips. “We work in people-watching central…if we don’t spot him there, where will we?”

“You know, I’m not quite sure I want him to be.” She took a sip of her coffee, as she idly studied the peeling paint on the wooden bench they were sat on. They were both a little earlier than they normally were. It was unusual to get a free bench at the station. It had started to rain since Sasha got there though, and that usually had an impact on the number of people who chose to drive to work instead of catching the train. Sasha caught Leigh’s confused expression.

“Look, Leigh, at the moment, he’s… an imaginary figure. He’s pretty perfect.” Sasha stopped for a moment, remembering certain physical aspects that always sent her into a quiver. “And…he’s not there in the morning.” Sasha shrugged.

Leigh snorted and tried her best to recover her stature as some of her coffee came through her nose. They both knew, on pain of death by their supervisor Mina, they should present a professional image and pay attention to their deportment at all times when in uniform, even when not actually on duty.

Sasha continued “What if he turns up at check-in one day and looks totally the part, and then turns out to be a complete douche…?” She lowered her voice as she reached the last word, checked that no one was stood too near them, and continued, “…or, just has a tiny dick…” to which Leigh almost choked on her drink again. Sasha grinned at her and raised her cup to drink again.

"Christ Sash!" Leigh exclaimed, changing the subject, looking at Sasha's hand as it gripped her cup. "Mina's going to have your hide if you go in like that! Better stop at Boots on the way in."

Sasha passed her cup to her other hand and inspected her fingernails. There were chips on two of her fingers and another was almost completely bare. Bugger. She was rostered to check in the afternoon's holiday charter so even in this weather she couldn't even hide them under gloves by staying airside. Half an hour in the toilets would be required, removing the damaged manicure, to ensure 'a suitably uniform appearance' as per the uniform handbook.

She chastised herself, all because a few slithers of coral polish had come off when she was doing housework yesterday. Well, at least following uniform regulations meant they were more likely to be best presented if and when Mister Right turned up at their check-in counter or boarding gate. Even if she wasn't as well-decorated as some of her colleagues, make-up wise.

Of course, he never did. Mister Right had yet to appear. More often than not he was replaced by Mister "I'm always right" holding up the queues of frequent travellers checking their watches.

The train finally pulled in to the station and Sasha jumped on. It was a moment or two before she realized Leigh wasn't next to her. Sasha momentarily panicked until she turned to see Leigh rushing towards her from the small newsagent booth at the end of the platform.

Leigh jumped on just as the door-closing alarm was sounding, smiling and holding out a small pink bottle.

"They sell nail polish remover...who knew?!" Leigh announced, gleefully. Sasha grinned back, a small sense of relief mingling with a sense of appreciation of having a friend to lean on. Literally, for a moment, as the train pulled out of the station and Leigh jerked forwards, almost pushing Sasha into the quite unimpressed besuited businesswoman behind her. Sasha nodded an apology at the woman and the two girls tentatively stepped down the carriage to find a seat for the rest of their journey.

2

Once again, like she did every morning, Sasha glanced up and down the row of check-in desks from the walkway behind, checking they were relatively tidy, empty bins, the relevant open desks had boarding passes and baggage labels loaded into the printers, and those desks that weren't being used this morning were empty. They didn't want to be slapped with a fine for leaving security-sensitive paperwork within reach of the public. They had it drummed into them that they would be held responsible for any consequences should anyone be able to get hold of official boarding passes or baggage tags, and use them for unofficial, or worse, nefarious purposes.

Once she was satisfied, she made her way to her assigned check-in, to make herself comfortable. She signed in to her various computer systems; since it was inevitable she'd be checking in multiple airlines and onward flights today and a few liked to use their own systems. She smiled as Lucas, one of the new intake of passenger service staff, sat on the desk next to her. He was eager to learn, and was quite a good learner to boot, so being assigned to mentor him wasn't too much of a task. Plus, he was funny. He made a point of checking out every single person who passed from their prime people-watching positions and giving her his opinions and 'marks out of 10'. So far, Sasha had gathered that his tastes were extremely wide-ranging and eclectic.

Her attention wandered slightly, noting the rest of the check-in agents systematically taking their seats along the row of desks, as Lucas continued to describe, almost to himself, a rather buff-looking taxi driver he could see through the glass front of the terminal building in front of them, who was unloading some luggage onto the pavement.

Sasha and her colleagues all had their own reasons for working at the airport. Most fell for the initial attraction of the perceived glamour of the industry – bygone eras of pert air hostesses with matching physical profiles and blood-red lipstick, dripping off the arms of picture-book handsome airline pilots. Some fell by the wayside soon after realizing the reality of 20-hour days (unending if the delays were indefinite and the next shift came in but couldn't relieve as they had their own scheduled flights to deal with) and blistered feet, and 5 spare pairs of tights in your handbag in case of the inevitable ladders from pushing wheelchairs whilst holding the poise of a supermodel in 3inch heels; and being raked across hot coals and threatened with the Department for Transport, or DfT, if you forgot to ask the 'security questions. Of course everyone knows those. The questions that recur as constant fodder for stand-up comedians.

Those that remained in the job, or were enticed for the travel aspect, got hooked on the adrenaline, the promise given by the constant departures of airplanes, of actually going somewhere someday like the people who came and went and forgot about you as soon as they boarded; the thrill of being closer to an aircraft than they'd ever imagined; the odd thrill of having the freedom to come and go through doors that usually remained locked to the greater population of traveling public. Some stayed where they were for a long time; forgetting that time passed; still dreaming the same dream each day, being a constant and stalwart face around the place.

Sasha herself had been here for 7 years. Theirs was a relatively small airport in the grand scheme of things. Not a massive hub, with millions of regular commuters a year. It was much smaller, one main terminal, a handful of 'airbridges' – the drivable walkways that attached to the side of larger aircraft. They were well located. A coastal spot, meaning they had clearer weather than some other 'regional' airports. This was a bonus sometimes; fewer weather related delays and cancellations when the sea air cleared away fog and mist and held the occasional ice and snow at bay.

On the other hand, it also meant they were a well-used diversion point. When other airports had to close because of weather, invariably, they'd be where the stranded airborne flights headed to land. The overtime up for grabs (and sometimes, demanded), to await the arrival of the extra flights, meant organizing buses, ticket alterations, compensation and a myriad of other arrangements for the diverted passengers- all while bearing the brunt of the blame for the diversion, and any subsequent problems. Sasha had experienced the sheer excitement, the fun and magic of the place in her early seasons, and had thought she had seen it all.

Until, that was, the massive, scary upheaval caused by the devastating events in the USA on September 11th, 2001. She had watched that on TV at home, aghast.

She had worked a standard, uneventful early shift that morning, packing off a flight full of holidaymakers to a tourist hotspot. She had been at home in bed by 9am; waking up, spookily, just as the first plane hit the first tower in New York City.

Her brother had been staying over after a night out; he'd called upstairs "A plane just flew in to the World Trade Centre". A shout in itself that hadn't aroused much suspicion – a bit of smoke, she expected, the corner of a floor or two smashed up, by a small 2-seater with a single pilot on board who'd had a heart-attack at the controls, maybe? That happened. Unfortunate that he was flying over Manhattan at the time, though.

She made a cup of tea before sitting down in the living room and turning on the TV. She was just in time to see the second plane hit the second building.

"There's no way that was an accident – One, maybe, but not two. See ya later, Sis, thanks for the sofa." Her brother had said, on his way out through the front door.

The TV coverage held Sasha mesmerized for the rest of

the day, as it had the whole world.

Her own little world, in her small town, was a million miles away from the events; she still knew it would have a ripple effect, connotations for her and her work family. Because that's what they felt like. Interspersed with the images she saw on the TV, she flashed back to their parties, nights out, special occasions, 'down-time' fun around work while waiting for flights. Shift work sometimes leaves people unable to socialize in 'normal hours' with friends and family from outside work, who had regular, 9 to 5 type jobs; so it made more sense to socialize with those working the same shift patterns; so invariably, social life and work life were intertwined. Not to mention, their favourite, most comfortable 'haunt' was a small, tired-looking, diner-come-bar along the airport ring road, called "Landing Lights", after its location, which doubled as a sort of airport social club. It was owned and run by one of the baggage handlers, Francois, known as Frenchy, and his wife; which kind of automatically made it part of the airport 'family' in its own right.

They had no direct flights to the USA operating from the airport. Come to think of it, they dealt with small feeder flights; they had no flights longer than 3 hours, tops. For an outsider looking in, it shouldn't have been any different for them at all.

Sasha had called the office, and offered to go back in. She had a dreaded feeling, hearing US airspace was closed completely, that planes would soon start dropping out of the sky.

She was right. A multitude of diverted flights that had been innocently and unknowingly heading across the Atlantic flight paths, as scheduled, at the time of the attack, had suddenly been contacted by their nearest Air Traffic Controllers and told to turn back, with little explanation; only then to be told they couldn't go back to where they had originated, because everyone else already had… Heathrow, Gatwick, Manchester, everywhere started filling up with the flights that were grounded having been ready to take off, and the flights that had already taken off having to return.

These massive jet liners were being distributed out to the smaller, less equipped airfields because there was no way they could go back to where they came from; and it was the unsuspecting staff at these small airfields who got it in the neck from the passengers, also innocents, who were all oblivious to the catastrophic events on the other side of the world. No one knew why, or how long, whether passengers should be disembarked or repatriated, or what to do with them if they did.

There would never be enough hotel accommodation for the people in transit from other countries let alone those who lived hours away. People who hadn't started here were transiting and had no visa or visitor permit so Immigration officers were snowed under. Catering outlets struggled to cope with requests for refreshments for the millions of stranded passengers. Chaos ensued and remained for days and even weeks to follow; right down to filing the paperwork – countless MATOs (pronounced 'may-tow', stood for Meal,

Accommodation and Transportation Order – a sort of invoice used by airports to book those things en masse in the event of disruptions), piles of Flight Interruption Manifests (FIMs) piling up on the ticket desk; and reuniting the hundreds of misloaded and uncollected luggage with the disgruntled owners.

Sasha had cried herself to sleep that first night, whether from stress, or relief at being able to go home, or maybe a little more affected than those who had families and other things to worry about. Sasha was a single girl who lived alone. Her workplace was her everything; her colleagues were also her friends, her social circle.

She somehow knew that place was about to change drastically, forever.

By this time, the following Sunday, traditionally a quiet day flight-wise after the Summer season closed down, Sasha and Leigh finally managed a sit down on the apron, waiting for the Jersey shuttle to arrive back before they could close down for the day and head home. It was an unusually calm day for September. The rain showers of the morning had passed and the sun had managed to make the afternoon bearable. They hadn't had a chance to chat properly for over a week – unusual for them. They hadn't even had after-work drinks at Landing Lights for more than 2 weeks. Frenchy was probably wondering where they were.

Frenchy, as it happened, had been having an unusually quiet week himself. The subdued feeling of shock coupled with exhaustion of trying to get the backlog back to normal had meant most of his clientele hadn't much felt like a Landing Lights type of night. And he hadn't blamed them.

"So, how's that family history research going?" Leigh probed, "any closer to anything useful?"

"It's not really. I was thinking of heading down to the West Country to search out that farm that Great uncle Owen told us about. Feel like getting away and Cornwall's always popular I'm told." Sasha replied.

"Popular? Understatement! Everyone goes to Cornwall for holidays. That Newquay gets popular." Leigh pointed out a turbo prop parked up on stand 3.

It had started doing regular flights down to Newquay airport and was regularly full of yuppie surfers.

"Apparently this farm is down near St Just. Think I went there for a holiday once when we were young. Before Uncle Myles moved away we all used to go on hols together with my cousins."

Sasha had vague memories of singing '*Summer Holiday*' along with the radio, driving down in convoy and staying in holiday chalets smelling of beaches and cleaning fluid; and singing '*Puff the Magic Dragon*' around a campfire on the sand in the darkness.

Sasha mused, sharing pinpoints of memories with Leigh, a faraway look in her eyes at the mere thought.

"Aww I love Cornwall." Leigh joined in. "Get over to

Land's End for a look too. Bit touristy but OK. Can make believe you're in a Daphne du Maurier book, sometimes when the weather gets blowy. If you're that way inclined. Old romantic like you shouldn't have any problems." Leigh winked at her friend. Sasha had always been one for being windswept and interesting.

"Here it is" Sasha pointed to the outline of an aircraft in the distance, barely visible above the housing estate at the end of the runway. The girls stood up, ready to call it landed and escort the passengers across the apron. "Why is he flying so low?" queried Leigh.

"Captain Bowen noticed something wrong with the cabin pressure or something earlier. Decided what the hell, he could still go if he flew below a certain flight level all the way there and back after he checked the passenger loads and knew he could take enough fuel."

"Nutter!" snorted Leigh, shaking her head at the thought of the jolly ex-RAF pilot who was nearing retirement, enjoying his final years of flying locally. As the tiny aircraft taxied towards them, before the noise got too much and their ear-plugs were their only barrier, Leigh hit on the idea they could make a trip of it.

"We'll all go down together, maybe in a minibus – remember Neil and Anya's day-trip to Alton Towers for their birthdays? That was fun!" Sasha smiled, although wondered if it wasn't a trip she wanted to do alone, and pretend to be romantic and dreamy for a while.

3

Sasha didn't get around to arranging her Cornwall trip until the following March. She had so much leave saved up she thought about taking it all in one go. Apart from a few days over Christmas to spend with her mum, most of the rest of her time off was arranged through shift swaps.

Sasha lived alone in a small, rented, 2-bed terrace, and one train stop away from work. She had had enough of living with her mum after backpacking around the USA, having worked a summer camp abroad programme; but managed to stick it for a little while longer.

After a few months of working extra shifts she'd saved up enough for the deposit and bond on a cheap rental – run down and questionable foundations; but freshly painted to make it look presentable enough. She figured she could just about manage it; especially for the excitement and experience of living alone for the first time.

She had been there 6 years and quite liked it; not having to answer to anyone and doing everything her own way. It just got lonely sometimes. Lying alone, in bed; or watching TV on her own. All the time, while her friends and colleagues worked different shifts or else had families of their own to occupy them. She booked the one week off work, with a day or two either side of her planned stay in Cornwall so she didn't feel like rushing – it was to be her first proper holiday in a while after all. Despite Leigh's insistence they make a group trip of it; they couldn't decide a suitable coinciding date; and those who were interested were unable to all book time off together anyway.

Sasha shrugged Leigh's plans off and insisted she'd prefer to go it alone initially. It was more her quest for knowledge of her family history she was going for anyway, not a drunken jolly. Leigh reluctantly allowed her to go on the promise that she'd save a couple of weeks of leave for a proper summer holiday. On the third Monday in March, Sasha boarded the train at the station for the first time, heading in the opposite direction from the local lines carriage to work. The Intercity 125 was far more luxurious, even the cheap Apex fare she'd bought.

Maybe not Business class airline experience, but she was quite happy watching the British countryside go by at high speed in the relaxing spring sunshine with some easy listening pop tunes shuffling on her MP3 player; thumping into her ears from her earphones, keeping her mood light and cheery and holiday-minded.

The views as she passed through the counties…Avon & Somerset, onwards through Devon and finally crossing in to Cornwall reminded her of the early morning banter on the radio, favourite DJs her mum always used to listen to, reminiscing about Devonshire teas and

Cornwall. It seemed so much sweeter with the sun shining on it too. Little white sailing boats bobbing on water outlets that glistened with sunbeams; cliffs rolling into slightly choppy but glistening seas; green fields and vast expanses of moorland seemed a brighter shade in the sunshine; even motorways looked sexy in this weather – stretches of asphalt snaking through the land with glinting metal and glass catching the rays as the train sped past.

By the time the train reached the end of the line in Penzance, she was in a beautifully relaxed mood. She'd packed light; having not intended to do much apart from tramp around the countryside and get a feel for this magical place her ancestors roamed, that she'd read about in romantic old books.

Penzance train station was like a scaled down version of the big old stations across the UK. Reminiscent of old times when trains were king and took everyone on their trips to the seaside; or off to war, or boarding school, or anywhere vaguely important or exciting.

Sasha almost felt like she was in some old movie. She smiled as she took her takeaway coffee from the platform refreshment stand and headed towards the exit; envisioning a kind of Hogwarts Express starting here before stopping at its platform 9 ¾ pick-ups in London and onwards to Hogwarts. She exited into the car park and taxi stand to an onslaught of bright sunshine and seaside aromas – the sea air, the fish market nearby on the quayside; and the sound of a multitude of gulls and the captivating view of St Michael's Mount off the coast to the east.

Sasha was in no hurry to end her journey. More often than not, she preferred the very act of traveling, enjoying the journey itself, to the destination and whatever relaxation and peace that offered.

She took the afternoon to wander up the quaint town centre and grab a few necessities from the big pharmacy and general store on the high street; some postcards for the girls and her mum and brother.

After sampling a Cornish pasty from the bakery Leigh had told her to go to, which, she concluded, could have been one of the best meals she had ever had; sat on the quay side in the sun, cooled by gentle seashore breezes; ogled by sea birds after any crumb she left behind; Sasha sought out the small bus that serviced the end of the peninsula, the south coast villages via Newlyn, down towards Land's End, then back up the North coast from Sennen through St Just and back into Penzance.

Her initial destination was a tiny speck of a fishing village not 3 miles from Newlyn; called Tregiffen. As the small bus with its 5 occupants rattled down the steep cliff track towards the village, Sasha mused that this could have been hundreds of miles from anywhere. Even a 3 mile walk to Newlyn would be a struggle up this hill.

She had settled on this place purely by doing an internet search for accommodation and chosen by location from pins on a map.

The Sailors Rest was a small tavern Inn from what she

could gather, with a few good reviews.

Very few, for it seemed very few visitors ever came through here, even fewer stayed. Given the terrain this village was nestled amongst, sheltered from the outside world by immense cliffs in every direction but out to sea, this was not a practical place to use as a tourist base for exploring. Even with a car she would have risked some kind of suspension damage with the state of the roads.

Sasha alighted from the bus, thanking the driver with a nod. It trundled on out of the village with no other passengers stopping here Ah well, Sasha mused, I'm here now, better make the best of it.

With a deep breath, which initially made her gag a little at the strong stench of fish guts and bait from the nearby quay – which, she noticed, was far smaller than Penzance and had no form of pleasure cruisers or tourist trip boats moored – this was a working place purely and simply, no time for relaxing cruises or cow-towing to holidaymakers – Sasha looked around for a road sign, or something, at least, to show her the location of the inn. No such luck. And the entire place seemed deserted.

The clatter from behind her signalled the presence of a young man, perched on a wooden step-ladder attempting to clean windows along the sea front. He had clumsily tipped the tin bucket he was using, and in his frustration was teetering atop the rickety perch.

Sasha lunged towards him and helped steady the ladder.

The youth spied her with initial distrust, which abated a little when she smiled a "hello" smile at him. "Ta" he muttered in the tone of an adolescent trying not to admit he'd made a mistake.

"No probs" Sasha replied, trying her best to avoid any type of condescending remarks. He couldn't have been more than 15 or 16. Maybe, she thought, helping out the neighbours for a bit of pocket money.

"Can you help me?" Sasha asked, "I'm supposed to be staying at a place called The Sailors Rest on Admiralty Rise, but I can't see any road signs around."

The boy indicated with his head up the nearest hill.

"Up there and on this side" He murmured.

"Thanks. I'm Sasha. "She held out a hand. He took it, weakly.

"Ned" he nodded. His manner was that of someone who had been ordered in no uncertain terms to be polite to strangers and visitors on pain of a good hiding from an adult, begrudged the requirement but did it all the same.

"See you around Ned, thanks again!" Sasha smiled sweetly at him and scurried off in the direction he gave her.

Sasha smiled as she entered the dark, dingy but strangely homely bar, to be faced with the portly landlady.

"Hi, uhm, I'm looking for James Andrewartha?"

"Sasha? " The landlady enquired. Sasha Nodded.

"James's my husband. Welcome to Tregiffen!"

"Thanks" she replied "quiet around here, isn't it?"

"Ah well that's true. We don't get many visitors. Las' newcomer round 'ere was a fisherman joined Ol'George's crew an even that was 3 years ago. Follow me love,"

"Thanks Mrs…"

"Call me Martha." the woman replied.

Sasha, amused, giggled a little involuntarily. "Your name is Martha Andrewartha? "

"Can't choose who you fall in love with, eh? " Martha replied with a twinkle in her eye.

Sasha just smiled in response, all the while thinking 'I wish I knew' to herself. Martha chatted away, while leading Sasha along the narrow corridor with ancient beams and creaking floors.

"Here you go, room 2. Weren't sure if you were bringing someone, and wanted twin beds or a double. This 'un's got a queen size, nice view of the cove." They reached the room and Martha opened the door, holding the door open for Sasha to enter first.

"Just me." Sasha smiled. She glanced quickly around the room. "View is good. Thanks Martha, "she said as Martha handed her the key, on a ring with a huge, hand-made wooden key-fob with her room number carved into it.

"Anything else you need let me know." the jovial middle-aged lady quipped as she waved a well-worn hand and backed carefully into the small corridor, pulling the door closed as she went.

Sasha looked around approvingly at her accommodation. Extremely floral, painted almost blindingly bright white with a wallpaper border around the top and the middle of the wall emblazoned with blue, yellow and red flowers and green leaves. A window-seat had been built in under the wide bay window, to make the most of the stunning view of the village and the quay and across the small bay, out to sea, no doubt.

The window-seat itself, however, had been upholstered with the same material as the curtains – an off-white, cream colour patterned with multi-coloured flowers intertwined with snaking ivy vines. The Queen bed in the centre of the room was once again a clash – having been dressed with a lovely linen set Sasha could have sworn she'd seen once at her Grandmothers, before she passed away. Pale pink with yet another, totally different floral pattern from the walls and the curtains.

Apart from the wildly tasteless décor, the room was clean, and smelled fresh and the windows so spotless there could have been no glass there at all. The solid shelf in the corner containing a small kettle and an assortment of tea and coffee sachets was well stocked and showed that Martha really did care about the little things, and looked after the place well. Sasha lay down on the bed to check, and was pleasantly surprised to find it one of the most amazingly comfortable things she'd ever laid down on. At least, she told herself, when I turn out the light and forget about the flowers I won't have a problem sleeping. Or so she thought.

After her long journey and the walk around town, Sasha as getting tired, even though it was only just nearing 6pm. After freshening up and digging out her nightclothes from her bag ready for later, Sasha opted for a walk around the village. She assumed that, from what she'd seen on her journey in, wouldn't take too long.

She was right. Roughly a 20 minute walk later she had completed a circuit. There was a small general store which, apart from the Inn, the only commercial outlet of any kind she could see. Seeing as it seemed to also serve as a post-office, bakery, hardware store and stationers, they appeared not to need much more within the confines of the village. And it was closed.

Sasha smiled to herself at the peculiarity of it all compared to her 'real' life. She meandered along the quayside for a while listening to the water lapping at the bottom of the boats. Not that there were many. A few small row boats, some were beyond use.

There were two smaller fishing boats with proper cabins on them; and one larger one, seemingly more commercial. Still not massive, but looking like the largest boat that could be occupied in this small marina.

The whole place was quiet. She saw not a soul on the street at all during her walk.

Out to sea she could barely make out one yacht sailing past the cove, further out to sea, as the light faded. Apart from that, there was nothing, not even a cat in the street.

Returning to the Inn she found the place quite lively. Every occupant of the village must be in the small bar – packing it tightly so that she could barely make it from the door to the bar. Martha from behind the bar saw her almost immediately, and waved her over to a table in the corner. Sasha sat down on the heavy upholstered bench that ran along the wall, dark oak table in front of her and on the next table, four or five heavy set fishermen. From the smell of them they hadn't been home since being out on their boat that day, a heady combination of fish remains, pipe tobacco and alcohol. She smiled openly at them as they cheerily bade her welcome to their village, all apart from a sullen, balding one in the corner and a dark bearded one, whose eyes, barely visible below the mop of hair that fell below his beanie hat, or above the massive bushy beard that hid the rest of his face, narrowed suspiciously at her.

All of them around the table seemed like something from a pirate novel, swigging back beers or shots of rum, laughing loudly about something one of them grunted – being unfamiliar with the accents she could make neither head nor tail of what they were saying; but felt it polite to smile in agreement or nod along at random points. She felt all at once that judging a place by stereotypes was not always wise, but from the looks of the rabble in the bar this evening, it was difficult not to.

The noise in the bar was so deafening it was difficult to make out anything, but when Martha brought out a bowl of hot soup and crusty bread and placed it carefully in front of Sasha, and tried to explain what was in it, Sasha smiled to show she was grateful for it, whatever flavour it turned out to be. She tucked hungrily into it, and although still unable to pinpoint what flavour it was supposed to be, it was warm, tasty and very welcome after her long day.

At one point during her ravenous demolishing of it, she had glanced up and was pretty sure the bearded fisherman had been staring at her; but if he had been he glanced away as quickly as she looked up. The suspicion was enough to make her take care with her table manners and finish the meal with a little more decorum than she otherwise would have, had she not suspected being watched.

When she finally climbed the narrow, creaky staircase to her floral room, she was exhausted. She spent a few minutes scribbling basics like "Lovely here, see you soon" or "Wish you were here" on the back of the postcards she'd bought in Penzance, the collapsed into bed. It was an inevitable truth of postcard-sending that unless you posted them as soon as possible into your holiday, you were more than likely to arrive home before they were delivered.

Sasha found she was right about the comfort of the bed and her need for a good rest. After the lights went out;

she slept better than she had in a long time. The dream returned, however, and by the time she awoke the next morning her crotch was, once again, soaking.

4

On Tuesday morning Sasha woke with the sun. She lay in silence for a while, enjoying the peace, broken only by the cackle of sea gulls outside. She mused she could really imagine herself living by the sea. She found her hand idly rubbing gently across her breasts, arousing her nipples under her pyjama top, down across her stomach and slowly in between her thighs, closing her eyes and thinking of the dream, imagining herself and her lover living by the sea, making love every morning as the sun came up to the sound of the birds.

Realising she'd really need to wash her PJs before wearing them again this evening she sat up in bed and made a mental note to ask Martha about a launderette or something nearby.

She grabbed her wash bag and crept along the corridor to the shared bathroom. She had no idea if Jimmy and Martha slept here or whether there were other guests, but better be safe than sorry; and made a mental note to double check with Martha about other residents next time she saw her.

Sasha locked the door carefully and took a quick shower and crept back to her room. Realising she'd forgotten to bring her make up bag she made the best with the emergency mascara in her handbag and her lip balm.

The room, she found, was also lacking in a hair dryer. Hardly worth waking Martha up for though, she brushed her towel-dried, mid-length hair through and left it to hang over her shoulders and down her back to dry, and slung a scrunchie around her wrist to tie it back with later.

Sasha checked herself in the mirror. It was actually a relief to find she didn't look too bad with the 'au naturel' look. She spent so much of her daily life at home either made up to a suitable standard to perpetuate the glamour of her industry; or else getting dressed up to the nines for nights out with the gang; for they were never quick drinks down the pub, it invariably turned in to heading on to the clubs in the city until the early (or not so early) hours of the morning. Yes, 'forgetting' her make-up bag might well have been a purposeful accident; and certainly a bit of relief for her skin, to say the least.

From the window of her room, Sasha'd seen the largest fishing boat that she'd noted last night, come in and moor at the quay. They must have left a long time before dawn to be returning already. She dug her camera from her case and threw it in her shoulder bag. The sunlight was perfectly placed for some beautiful shots of the cove and the quayside, the quaintness of the village.

After a quick round of toast served by Jimmy behind the bar as she passed, Sasha half walked, half skipped back down the steep road towards the dock.

The high cliffs rising on either side of the natural cove were a dauntingly claustrophobic; yet at the same time reassuringly safe. It struck Sasha they must offer excellent protection from rough seas and wild weather. Thinking of it that way, she'd never seen the quaint fishing boats and stereotypical old fishermen she'd seen in pictures in such a light before, but these men must be very brave. Unsung heroes who never got as much coverage or glamour as the likes of soldiers and firemen did.

Sasha wandered along the quayside. The sun was in just the right position to be glistening on the water at mid tide; and the colours of the seaweed and the brightly painted rowboats, and buoys and ropes that scattered the whole area were conjuring up some brilliant photo opportunities for her and her amateur photography inclinations; but made her wish she could paint and create some of those old art-works she seen on hotel and pub walls.

The boat that came in earlier was moored up now, and being unloaded. Then hustle and bustle created by the crew seemed to make the whole village come alive compared to the desolation she had felt the evening before; even though she could count on one hand the number of workers she could see.

The one who seemed to be captain was supervising as the young boy who had been cleaning windows earlier, Ned, was stacking up what seemed to be to Sasha's untrained eye, a very good catch. There were numerous cages of crabs; quite a few crates of huge, fresh fish. The crew member who was passing the crates off to Ned was immense in size. Sasha watched him effortlessly haul the crates and hold them until Ned had a good grip. When the large man let go, Ned visibly stooped to hold on to it and stack it with the others.

The Captain noticed Sasha watching them.

"Mornin, Miss. Can we 'elp ya? "He called.

Sasha smiled and snapped out of the trance held by the large fisherman's abilities. She was for some reason very pleasantly surprised to recognise him from the next table the night before.

"Oh, no, thanks. I'm fine. I'm just visiting. This is my first time in Cornwall. Or anywhere near a real fishing boat." She explained, eyes bright with interest. He continued working and listening to her at the same time. "Just marvelling, normally don't see it till it's in batter at the chip shop." She finished.

"in 'at case, come 'an 'ave a proper look. " The captain offered jovially. He had neared her by now, and held out a calloused hand, removing his thick industrial glove.

"Cap'n George Oats. They call me ol'George round ere

though."

"Sasha Pender" she smiled. "Can I take a few photos? "

"Pender? Cornish are ye? "he inquired

"Apparently. I came down here to do a bit of family research. "

"From London?" He squinted at her, possibly trying to place her accent.

"God no, South Wales" she told him. He appeared to relax a little.

"I see. You'll be the one staying at the 'Rest' then." He stated, not sounding as though he wanted an answer. "So, photos? Some kind of Journalist are ye? "

"Huh?" Sasha's attention snapped back to ol'George again. She'd been mesmerised by the arms of the large crewman again.

"Oh, uhm, no. Just amateur photography. I wanted some really nice pictures to take back from my holiday with me and this is all so…quaint."

"Ha if you say so missy!" ol'George chortled. "Come on 'en, come see some of the crew."

Sasha followed ol'George towards the vessel. "Claudia's " name on the bow was faded but on the whole the boat seemed well loved and cared for; even to Sasha's untrained eye. She was a fairly good sized boat, and Sasha mused this must be good full-time work for the men on Ol'George's crew. There seemed to be four of them on board in all; in addition to ol'George, the large one offloading the crates to Ned, There was a bald, strong looking seaman sweeping the deck at the back of the boat. He looked up and offered a kind of half-salute to Sasha as George as Derek.

" 'e's been wi'me for almost 20 years now. 'I'm and Steve Penrose. Steve's down below."

Steve appeared as if on cue from the cabin, wiping oil and grease from his hands, muttering under his breath.

"Georgy boy," he began "I'm gonna have to get to the shop and get some more oil and a replacement..." he stopped when he saw they had a visitor. "Ah, morning..." Steve nodded at her, averted his eyes. He jumped down from the ship onto the quay deftly, with all the confidence and skill of someone who'd been doing so for years. He scurried away still wiping his hands, climbed into a battered old banger and drove away.

"A bit shy he is. Old and stuck in 'is ways." Ol'George smiled. "Now then, want us to pose or anythin for some of yer pictures?" His eyes twinkled with excitement at the thought of being famous in some photos.

"Actually, no, I just thought I'd take some photos while you went about what you were doing..." Sasha said.

She noticed George's dejected expression. He must've been in his sixties, a little older than the others; she assumed them to be fiftysomething maybe, Derek maybe a little younger, late forties possibly. But George's disappointment manifested itself in his face so much as to make him seem like a chastised schoolboy.

The last crewman, the strong one on the deck who was unloading with Ned, with the dark hair and beard, she'd noticed last night, and had yet to be introduced, was watching George intently. Or seemed to be. Sasha felt his stare burning into her. When she looked up at him he didn't break the stare, he merely seemed to make it known with his expression that he wouldn't take kindly to being photographed himself, so to concentrate her camera on George.

"But on the other hand, you are a very good advert for your trade, George. I don't suppose you have a pipe at all?" Ol'George grinned and scurried off to the harbourmaster shed, returning minutes later with his pipe in hand, and tobacco pouch along with a box of matches. As he set about stuffing his pipe, revelling in his starring role, he looked up at Derek.

"Del boy. I'm thinking you should take this delivery along with Ned today. I'm gonna want Col to finish up some things around 'ere this morning."

Ned frowned at ol'George, giving Sasha the impression that this was either not a very welcome suggestion; or else a very unusual one, and that Ned knew his place enough to not question the Captain's orders, no matter how bizarre.

George turned back to Sasha, "This 'un's Colan. Newest crew member. "

"Three years ain't new, Cap'n" muttered Colan.

His accent and the sound of his voice threw Sasha off. She pondered suddenly that he may be slightly younger than all of them; both his hair and his extensive beard were black as coal, whereas even Derek's handlebar moustache had flecks of silver adorning it.

After the crates on the dock had been loaded on the awaiting flatbed truck, the still-confused Ned and a miserable looking Derek climbed in and disappeared off up the hill out of the village.

Ol'George explained to Sasha during his highly enjoyable photo shoot that they supplied a couple of the high end restaurants around the area; the kind set up to cater for the myriad of regular visitors from London and the surrounding areas; so they as a crew delivered directly to them the freshest stuff; then off to Newlyn and Penzance to get the highest price they could for the rest.

Col normally did it due to his being more in his prime and stronger than the rest at hauling the crates. Why George had decided to send Derek today, he didn't quite explain. Derek had tried to get an explanation out of him before leaving but the Captain had fudged over the details. Sasha got the impression that for some reason, George was trying his best not to say something in front of her.

After the truck left, there was almost an hour of Ol'George posing like a pro; his expression changing on cue to that of a serious, furrowed, hardened seaman; returning to a jovial, sunny excited child as soon as the shutter closed; on the boat, off the boat; with pipe, without pipe, holding a fish tail, pulling a rope.

Sasha thoroughly enjoyed directing this old man who revelled in the attention. At one point, she wondered if she had missed her calling and maybe she should look in to photography a little more seriously.

The entire time, Sasha knew they were being watched intently by Col as he went about his business; laying out nets to dry and checking for breaks; gathering ropes, generally clearing up after the morning's work.

Colan, for his part, was actually trying his best not to show too much interest. Since he'd arrived here 3 years ago, there hadn't been much in the way of female attention to vie for. He'd been running, of sorts, so was glad, not only not to have anything to distract him there; but for there to be no opportunity for his elders and peers, themselves already married and settled, to find suitable young ladies to try and "hook him up" with.

This visitor, although they'd heard she was only here for a week, felt like a danger to him. He couldn't help watching her; much as he tried to keep his head down. He wasn't sure if it was something about her in particular, or if his self-imposed dry spell had lasted so long now that any piece of half-decent skirt on the menu could have been a temptation.

Trying to only glance in their direction when her back

was turned to him, he figured she was late-twenties, maybe a little older the way women take care of themselves these days, mid-length blonde hair in a cutesy ponytail. Not a bad figure. Not stick thin by far, something to grab hold …

Right, now's the opportune moment to disappear below deck, he told himself. Wait until she's gone, eh, Col?

Ol'George, on the other hand, enjoying the sunshine and his moment of glory, had, of course, had his own reasons for sending Derek away and keeping Colan close.

His old, soppy self had come out when a young lady had arrived in the village, travelling alone by accounts from Jimmy at the 'Rest' who'd taken the booking, wearing no form of ring on her left hand.

George worried about his crew like a father on most occasions; his main reason for keeping Ned under his wing but having not let him out to sea with them just yet until he was old enough, strong enough and had perfected every piece of procedure on land first. He had trouble getting much more information out of Colan Tangye than the very basics, even after three years, but he knew this boy was a perfect catch for some lucky lady.

Strong, silent type, for the most part, hard worker, although he did disappear without a word or a trace a few too many times – no woman George knew of would put up with that. The right one could probably beat that habit out of him.

Up until now, however, George hadn't had much opportunity to test out any theories of a woman getting the catch on Colan Tangye. Since his arrival 3 years ago, apart from the odd tour group of Yanks and Europeans and some Londoners, passing through for a quick photo op on their way to Land's End; there hadn't really been any influx into the village.

Even socials at St Buryan and Sennen, and further afield, never seemed to throw up any opportunities. The options seemed to range from teenagers who had yet to leave town for college, straight to wives and mothers already, with nothing in between.

Now, here was his first chance. He bloody hoped Tangye would clean himself up for the occasion and make the most of the opportunity. So far George had been thoroughly disappointed with his lack of reaction. He'd be having stern words with the slow bugger, he would, later. He only had a bloody week to make a lasting impression! If only I were a few years younger myself, had been one of George's earlier thoughts, until he remembered his good years with his own wife, and pushed that out of his mind, labelling it as proof that this girl would be good for Colan.

Thank God she'd given them the most opportunity by coming down here on her first day. His hopes had begun to rise, however, when he caught the lad staring at the young lady when she wasn't looking – George facing her obviously had a great view of Col's green eyes boring a hole into her back. Had George allowed himself to be a bit more of an old romantic, he would have sworn he saw a twinkle of hope in them eyes.

Right, thought the Captain to himself, time to scarper I think. “Ok then, missy. I really need to be getting back to the Mrs who’ll have me dinner ready by now. I think you should get a bit of diversity into yer roll of film if you got a bit or the lad in there too. Can’t ‘ave the world thinkin’ all fishermen in Cornwall look like me!”

Sasha giggled a little at the thought – George was a little bit of a stereotypical old sea dog – cable knit sweater and sailors cap and long bushy white beard. Paint him blue and he would have been reminiscent of Papa Smurf.

“Colan, Come up a sec.” He paused as the large frame of Colan Tangye nimbly traversed the stairs from the cabin, crossed the deck in one bound and leapt expertly onto the quay.

Sasha let a small gasp of admiration escape, not so loud as to allow Colan to hear, but George grinned, since he had his back to Sasha. If you wanna impress a girl, my lad, there’s where to start.

“Colan I know you have stuff to do but if you wouldn’t mind letting the young lady have free reign down here – keep an eye on her safety mind you – so she can take some nice photos of me girl for me, eh?”

With that, as though not giving Colan a chance to protest, the old man scurried away into one of the cottages along the front of the quay. He quickly disappearing inside without a backwards glance. Sasha could have sworn she half saw him skip a few steps.

"Okay! Thanks for all the help." Sasha said, as though to the shadow of George as he disappeared. She turned to Colan, and took a deep breath, as though she needed extra courage to speak to him, not that she quite understood why.

"I get the impression you don't seem to want your photo taken?" Sasha said, lightly. She had no intention of sounding challenging, giving him any reason to be any gruffer than he seemingly was.

Tangye grimaced at her enthusiasm.

"Rather not," he grunted. Man of few words, then.

"I was wondering if it would be OK to get on board and take a few from different angles up there?"

Colan said nothing, he looked at her eyes. They were brown, but light and almost innocent, playful. Sasha wondered if he was going to say something. Seems not, she told herself. The awkward silence had to be broken by one of them.

"I think the Captain implied it would be OK, I mean, I just wondered if you could assist; hold my hand as I…got up?"

"Boarded?" he corrected.

"Yeah." She blushed. Shoulda known that, idiot!

He grabbed her wrist and almost tugged her up off the ground, surprising her so much she ended up right up close to his chest as she landed on the deck, coming almost face to face with him, had he not been that much taller.

She froze, after a tingle of electricity shot up her back making her gasp and parted her lips slightly, losing herself in the moment.

“Wanna know what it’s like to kiss a proper Cornish fisherman too eh?” he growled at her. What an odd thing to suggest, she pondered, as she suddenly recovered herself.

“I just wanted a picture. I just thought I could get something arty and evocative…”

All the same, she did wonder…No, Sasha! She told herself. A kiss from this ruffian would be like some drunken old uncle at Christmas.

She tried again to shake off the images that thought were conjuring in her mind before she gagged publicly.

Damn him, why on earth would he suggest such a thing, weird, old, repulsive man.

It was only then, as soon as she thought he wasn’t looking that she looked at him again, this time trying to see past the image of the salty sea dog, scruffy sea clothes, hat, beard, and look at his actual face.

To her surprise, he suddenly struck a very different figure. His face didn’t match her initial image of him.

He wasn’t leathery skinned, weathered by years at sea. The man beneath the exterior stereotype she had painted him as, and to be fair, that he was dressed as, couldn't have been in his 50s or 60s as she'd initially assumed. He had few lines around his eyes. A few laughter lines maybe – although imagining him ever having laughed enough to gain them was a little difficult. This man she was studying now, may have been slightly over 40. She frowned a little, even younger – mid 30s maybe? And actually, take the beard off and he could be....he almost looked like...

"Ahem" Coughed Tangye. Sasha realised she had been staring at him; for longer than could pass for general. Sasha recovered herself. OK, at least an offer of a kiss was a little less sleazy if it was from someone who wasn't old enough to be her grandfather. But still, the thought of getting close enough to the creature to smell the fish remains on his clothing all but repulsed her. Sasha recovered herself enough to take leave of the man.

"Look, I'm sorry" she flustered "I just wanted a few photos of my holiday. I think the batteries are gone anyway, I'll go and... thanks anyway..." Sasha scurried away along the quay like a schoolgirl separated from her tour group.

Colan watched her go and wanted to punch himself in the face. Offering to kiss her? How stupid can you get man?! He chastised himself. Something about her made him want to scream at her to not take everyone, him especially, at face value.

DO NOT GET INVOLVED, he told himself, even if she is just here for a summer fling. With any luck, he had gotten away with the throwaway kiss comment. She won't be wanting any kind of fling with this character he was making himself out to be. Good thing too. Colan had work to do. He had put too much time and effort to get this far on the past three years to throw it away just because he hadn't been near any attractive, available women in his age group since Sarah.

Sasha dumped her bag on the floor and flicked on the small kettle in her room. She perched on the sweet window bench covered in bright floral fabric and looked out over the quay. From here she could see the fisherman continuing about his business. She wondered if their encounter had had any effect on him whatsoever. From her perch she saw only a heavy set stereotype going about his business, loading nets onto his vessel. The sudden realisation that this man she had been so repulsed by at first glance what nothing she had first imagined was getting to her. The nagging feeling that her initial perception of someone, as a professional people watcher, could have been wrong, would not leave her alone; but neither would the image burned into her mind's eye of the deeply penetrating green eyes that had playfully mocked her from behind the big bushy beard and below the healthy mop of shining black hair that fell loosely over his forehead…..

Oh my God, Sasha chastised herself, what the hell am I thinking about? She realised her heartbeat had raised and perspiration was gathering on her forehead. Sasha decided to forgo the tea, ignored the boiled kettle and lay down on her bed. The early morning and the introduction to Col Tangye had been more than enough for one day. She decided she would go for a walk later on to clear her head, after checking from her bird's eye view that the boat had been abandoned for the day, to avoid bumping into him again. Sasha fell into the deepest sleep she'd had in a long time, interrupted only by her favourite dreams of beaches and fun and the dream man who was there to catch her. She revelled in staring out to sea, this time, as his massive strong arms snaked around her, his nose nestled in her hair drinking in her scent. Sasha was filled with the overwhelming desire to turn and kiss him passionately. As she did so, she gazed hotly up into her lover's face, noticing as she didn't think she had before, that his eyes were a piercing green. He lifted her effortlessly and laid her down in the sand. Sasha felt every touch, every stroke, and every emotion as his hands moved up her thigh under her dress, and she thanked heaven she was wearing no underwear at this precise moment… Sasha woke with a start, her heart pounding still, now deep stirrings in the pit of her stomach which for once she wished weren't there at all; knowing full well the face her subconscious had attached to her dream man was that of the repulsive, rude fisherman, Colan Tangye, down at the quay. Not so repulsive in her dream, which might have been what frightened her so much more. Sasha rushed around the room gathering a few pieces of clothing that looked like they could do with a wash – it might look odd if she was just washing her nightclothes after just one night's sleep – and bounded down the stairs to find Martha polishing the tables in the bar.

“ ‘Course, love. Pengelly’s store on the corner has a coin operated machine out the back…”she said at Sasha’s enquiry, “… but I can always…”

“Thanks a million!” Sasha interrupted her quickly and dashed out the door. She didn’t want Martha to be wondering about the washing either.

Sasha stood in front of the washing machine in the cramped room at the back of the convenience store she had found the afternoon before and stared at the jumble of colours tossing around inside; attempting to hypnotise herself out of deep thought.

She did the same through the drying cycle but it still didn’t work. Somehow it wasn’t working. Her mind would not wipe Col’s face – a version of it without his beard – out of her head. She wasn’t even sure the walk she had planned earlier was going to be of any help at this point either.

When she returned with her laundry to the inn, Sasha politely declined Martha’s offer of a good hearty dinner, claiming a little over-tiredness from the journey still. Martha nodded and made her a sandwich to take up to her room.

Sasha nibbled on the soft white bread as she sat on the window seat staring at the sea, before feeling the need to lie on her bed. Despite herself, Sasha found herself touching herself all over again, furrowing up her face and knowing full well who it was her subconscious wished was doing this for her. She changed into her night clothes – or rather, just the baggy top. She didn't feel like explaining herself if questioned as to why she was washing her PJ's every single morning… The rest of her night's sleep was nothing if not disturbed.

5

Sennen Cove, Sasha had been told, was a summer mecca for surfers, beach bums and refugees from London.

On Wednesday morning, Martha gave her a rough idea of the bus times and found it was the same one that brought her into town, went down to Land's End and back up to Penzance via Sennen Cove.

Sasha borrowed a towel from Martha, just in case. It was the end of March of course, but the sun had been unusually hot for the past few days all over the country. Global warming had some perks it seemed, odd weather spells at the wrong time of the year. Sasha didn't put it past herself wanting to brave an ankle deep paddle, at the very least.

She was pleasantly surprised to find the place buzzing with life. Not even the Easter holidays, and on a bright sunny day, plenty of people were populating the mile of golden sands, children building sandcastles; families sitting outside the beach café eating ice-cream. Couples drinking pints outside The Old Success Inn on the corner; surfers old and young chasing the glistening waves. Some scantily clad brave young things were splashing about; still others were soaking up the rays on beach mats.

After a hike up along the beach path behind the surf shack, which she found came out by the life guard hut, closed and boarded up out of season, Sasha began to feel suitably confident, and quite hot from the heat and the walk, to strip down and brave the water. Conscious of being there alone, she chose a little spot to leave her bag, between a few rocks, out of sight of passers-by who may take the opportunity to relieve her of her belongings. She took one last look around to check if anyone was watching, forever self-conscious, very glad, at least there was no-one who knew her here to see her.

Sasha stripped underneath the towel Martha had loaned her. She debated whether to take it down to the water with her; to cover up until the last minute. It was a toss-up between keeping covered up and risking the towel getting wet in the waves. She heaved in a deep breath, opted to leave the towel and remind herself with each step that no-one was interested in watching her; and even if they were noticing this lump trundling down the sand they wouldn't know her from Eve to taunt her anyway. Sasha was satisfyingly surprised at the pleasure the sea gave her, never one to shy away from the cold, Sasha was one who would run out meet a flight in just her blouse in the middle of December without stopping to put on her coat for the sake of customer service, being at the gate on time and not keeping people waiting. She sometimes preferred to be freezing cold than warm. This water wasn't freezing, but it gave her a thrill. Blushing slightly at the thought of if anyone she knew could see her, she felt shivers travel up her spine; her shoulders quiver a little and became very aware that her nipples had hardened and could be clearly visible through her one piece, low leg swimsuit. She managed waist depth and closed her eyes as the swell moved around her. She floated her hands out in the water that surrounded her and stayed there for goodness knows how long.

Before she knew it, she had the overwhelming urge to make a dive for it. She took a deep breath and plunged into the water, emerging with a start, hair soaked through and lungs drawing in air deeply as the cold shocked her through. She recovered from the dive and noticed some children screaming from the shallower waters. Looking around, she noticed they'd let go of a beach ball that was floating away. Disheartened at the thought of them watching a toy drift away and never seeing it again, she felt the need to do something. Forever a strong swimmer, she took off after it and caught it in no time. She managed to grab it, steady herself enough to let a little air out of it so she could grab hold of it and swim back with it.

Handing it back to the grateful gang, they persuaded her to join a kick about. What the hell, nowhere to be, no-one to tell me no, or laugh at me wobbling about, these kids just want to play. Sasha played her heart out until the children were called up for their pasty-tea by parents who had enjoyed them being out of their hair for a while.

She smiled and waved the children off, and with such a contented feeling, headed back up to find her towel and bag untouched, thankfully. She started to towel herself dry, looking around at the stunning cove she had never imagined existed on the shores of the UK.

Up in the car park overlooking the beach, Colan sat behind the wheel of his truck in the car park replayed over and over what he'd been privy too. That morning when the boat had come in and the day's low catch had been loaded on to the truck, they're decided it would be quicker to split the load. He took some up to the Land's End hotel for their evening menu, sold some to the "First & Last" and "The Old Success" down in the cove and then took the delivery over to The Beach restaurant overlooking Sennen Cove. Their own boat "Rosebud" had been out of action for a short while, and "Claudia" had been helping out keeping their menu operational.

As he climbed back into the driver's seat, Colan had suddenly noticed; as Sasha had; how busy the beach was today. Two giggly young women in wetsuits carrying surfboards like they'd never touched one before in their lives had walked past him; he watched them meet up with a surf instructor near the entrance to the surf school below the restaurant, and had a thought.

As he turned on the radio, some song about beautiful girls was playing and something stopped him short of starting the ignition. He leaned forward on the steering wheel, watching the young girls walk by; he noticed he hadn't been as interested in them as the new girl in town.

Something told him it wasn't lack of action that was making him interested in the first available girl that came along. Col sat for a moment, surveying the beach and its larger-than-average crowd on a sunny March day. All shapes and sizes had decided to make the most of the early hot spell. From lithe young things lying on the sand to the sporty types having a go at surfing; even some of the local surfer girls he's seen before – and not batted an eyelid even then. Even the family mums, young and old. There was enough cross section of society surrounding him today to catch the attention of someone who was only thinking about one thing.

Then he saw it. The thing he was thinking about. Or, rather, the 'who'. Sasha was laughing; carefree, alive, kicking a beach ball around with a bunch of children. Her hair was loose, damp, hanging around her shoulders, swinging around when she tackled one of the boys, laughing harder than they were.

It was only after watching her for a few minutes, realising he was almost smiling at the excitement of seeing her, the thrill of watching unseen, the selfishness of taking this moment to himself and the discomfort the feelings that were rising up through him; he realised he hadn't even paid attention to her physical self. He'd been somehow watching the aura that surrounded her. The pleasure he was experiencing from his clandestine actions were filling him with guilt but he kept looking anyway.

What the hell, he told himself, she's in public, she's not hiding anything. She wasn't wearing any flashy, miniscule bikini that hid nothing that was becoming more the fashion. Low cut legs and high-cut chest line of this thing was more practical than most he'd seen. Which honestly wasn't many in recent times, but looking round, she was the most modestly dressed of the swim-suit clad people on the beach today.

His thoughts the day before about her figure hadn't concerned him overly. He hadn't ever expected to get any closer to it; or have it displayed before him in this way. Kind of Bridget Jones and then some. He'd never thought he had a "type" but had assumed the skinny supermodel girls were supposed to be it.

He couldn't even remember what Sarah's "Type" was. He just remembered Sarah. In fact, he thought, in all his years, he'd had a few women. He didn't really think of any of them as having a "type", they were just each individual person, a whole being. At this moment looking at Sasha in her swimsuit, it occurred to him an excitement was building inside him that had little to do with the objectivity of looking at a body; more the whole package. He closed his eyes and hit his head a few times against his fists on the steering wheel. He was distracted by a vibrating of his mobile on the seat next to him. He read the text.

Contact, 8pm.

Shit, he thought. By the time he'd looked up again, she was gone. The children were sat near him on the picnic tables wrapped in towels eating pasties. Sasha emerged from the stone staircase that led up from the sand to the car park, waving at the children she'd been playing with, and headed off to the bus stop. She hadn't even accidentally glanced in his direction; but all the same he had such a shock he ducked down a little. He must've watched her sitting at the bus stop for a good ten or twenty minutes before checking the clock on the dashboard. Fuck, it's twenty to six…. His concern wasn't for his appointment at 8; more for her – he knew the last bus left here at 1722 on the dot. She'd be sat here all night, short of walking miles back across the peninsula.

Col swallowed his pride and emotions; and regained his gruff, dark, hidden disguise he'd created for himself. He started the engine and drove up to the bus stop, coming to a halt directly opposite her, and staring at her with a quizzical eyebrow raised sarcastically. Sasha stared back, looked around, and marched forward as he wound the window down.

"You know the last bus left 'ere more 'an twenty minutes ago?" When Col watched her face sink, dejected, he hated himself for hiding behind a cocky, sardonic disguise. He knew he couldn't hold it up much more, short of driving off and leaving her to her own devices; when he could so easily have her sitting so close to him in the cabin of his truck. He looked at her; his expression softened and cocked his head to beckon her to get in.

Oh God, should I? Sasha wondered. After last night… She stopped. He has no idea about last night. She had dreamed about him, in the most graphic ways possible, over and over again. And here he was, just being a gentleman, offering her a lift.

It would be rude not to… Sasha's face cracked into a massive, beaming smile that made him feel as though he could melt. She rushed round the vehicle and climbed in, tossing her bag over her shoulder into the storage area, like she belonged here. She threw the seatbelt around here and placed her hands primly in her lap. How fucking endearing, he sighed to himself. "Where to?" "Oh!" she gazed at him quizzically. "I assumed you'd just take me straight back to Tregiffen?"

"Way I figure it, you're not gonna get much exploring done round 'ere if you rely on the local busses. This truck an' me at a loose end for a bit. So, where to?" he repeated.

What the fuck am I doing, offering to spend more time than necessary with her?

Col reached in to the back seat and tossed a local AtoZ at her. "Oh! Thank you!" She smiled sweetly at him, again.

"Well, the family farm I was supposed to be looking for is supposed to be out by St Just, somewhere. Is that too far?"

"St Just it is then…"

She settled back into the passenger seat. They spent a little time driving round by the time they found an old farmhouse with her surname etched into the gatepost concrete. Colan shrugged and looked at her expectantly.

"OK, two minutes then" she said, jumping out of the car

and gathering the courage to knock on the door. Colan watched her walking carefully up the overgrown path, something made him wish he was walking with her, holding her hand. He watched her knock, and wait, and wait. She turned a little dejectedly and returned to the passenger seat.

“Eh never mind,” he said “at least we know where it is now”.

We, she thought, is he thinking he’s getting involved with my little search now? Sasha snuck another sideways look at him as he concentrated on reversing the truck from the small siding they had stopped in.

“You hungry?” he looked at her. The fading light was going fast. She wondered if it was a good idea to be stuck in a vehicle on lonely roads in the middle of nowhere with him for too much longer. He felt dangerous. Intriguing but dangerous.

“OK,” she heard herself say.

“Warrens Cornish Pasty from St Just then.” He said. He glanced sideways and grinned at her. Reassuringly, he hoped. Sasha, despite herself, grinned back, suddenly feeling a little more comfortable, and a lot safer in this truck than she would be anywhere else in the entire world. They sat in the small village square under a streetlight eating the traditional savouries he seemed to love. Sasha recalled she had once had a version of from a store near the airport but they’d been nothing like these huge mounds of steak and vegetables, wrapped in the most gorgeous pastry she'd ever tasted. She closed her eyes to savour the food. It tasted good, comforting, and homely.

Colan enjoyed watching her. He was smiling to himself as she nibbled slowly. How the hell could it be so sensual to watch someone eating, and eating something as boring as a bloody pasty at that.... Fuck, he checked his watch, quarter past seven.

"I gotta go..."

"Go? Now? " Sasha's face gave away her fear.

"I'll drop you back to Tregiffen," he explained, mistaking her worry for being abandoned far from her lodgings. "I got a meetin' to get to."

"Meeting? A fishing meeting? " she now looked confused.

OK, so that caught me off guard. "A different business meeting. Kind of a side-line I got going. Nothin' special"

They travelled in silence back to Tregiffen. Something in his voice had warned her that his explanation was final.

Not my business anyway, she thought, I don't know his business or how fishing is supposed to work. All the same, Sasha was quite partial to ol'George, Ned, locals in Tregiffen she'd not known much more than 24 hours. She hated to think they were being taken for some kind of ride. Colan pulled up outside the ‘Rest’. Sasha climbed out and turned towards him.

“Ummm…thanks for …dinner I suppose. It was nice”

“s’ok” he shrugged.

“Have a good…meeting” Col shot daggers at her, a warning to keep quiet about it. Sasha pursed her lips and slammed the door shut.

The truck drove away and Sasha had no idea how long she stood there watching him go, but the truck had long since disappeared over the hill before she turned to go inside.

Col Tangye glanced repeatedly in the rear view mirror as he drove away. She was still there. Again, still there. She’s still watching. What was the old adage? If she keeps watching, you’re in with a chance? Shit, he was going to be in trouble…

6

Sasha's alarm on her phone awoke her at 3 the Thursday morning. She checked the calendar application and found she should have been at work at 4am had she not taken leave. Shit! How annoying is that?! She chastised herself for not turning off the reminders. Ten minutes of tossing and turning later, Sasha realised she couldn't get back to sleep now.

After an hour of attempting to read the paperback she'd brought with her, she knew it was pointless to continue trying to concentrate on that either. At 4.30am she had had enough of pacing, tossing, turning. She dressed and grabbed her bag. Stupid, walking at this time of the morning, in a village so small there was nowhere to go. It was pitch black, too, no streetlights to speak of. There had never seemed any need for them down here. The council had tried once, but once they were damaged by the wild weather or the bulbs simply gone, no-one had bothered complain to get them replaced.

Sasha saw one light – down on the quay, "Claudia" was coming to life. Ol'George could be heard barking orders to the others, getting the nets ready. Ned wasn't present, but Sasha, approaching purely because of the lack of any other interesting sights around at this time of the morning, Derek and Steve and Colan preparing for an early morning out.

Colan noticed her coming. Take the lead then, he told himself, getting too close as it is, can't pretend to ignore her any more.

Sasha's heart jumped despite herself as she saw his perfect frame execute another perfect leap over the deck, alighting squarely on the dockside, with little more than a tap. There just had to be more to this man than your average lumbering, hard-working seaman.

It was dark; she could barely make out his outline, the dock light behind him. As she got closer to him, his face became more prominent although still in shadow. She had the opportunity, if only for a moment, to make out his eyes and nose and not have the big bushy beard a distraction from admiring the strong features of face.

I'm admiring him? She penalised herself. Don't tempt yourself even more, girl!

"Early one, Miss Pender?" He spoke quietly – as though with deference to the rest of the village, not wanting to disturb anyone.

Oh my God his voice is smooth, Sasha once again found herself finding things to fascinate her about the hulk of a man, standing at least half a foot over her, if not more.

"I left my alarm on my phone on work-time, and couldn't get back to sleep. I'm just out for a walk, and there's not much to see around here at this time of the morning."

"Morning missy!" nodded Ol'George, startling and interrupting both of them. To each of their separate indignation. She could have sworn he winked at her as he passed. He didn't stop to converse, seemingly feeling he should leave them to it.

"Mind if I hang around a bit and watch?" She asked Col after George had passed. Col shrugged.

"Guess so." He avoided her gaze and turned back to his work.

Sasha sat back on the old stone wall separating the quay from the main road and watched intently.

She was amazed she had never thought about how much work went into fishing. It all seemed so quaint to city dwellers and townies like her when she saw pictures and stock footage of fishing boats; and of course, no one these days ever thought about where their food came from, not really.

It was frozen from the supermarket, or ready made at a restaurant, and then she just assumed the restaurant went to the local fish monger and it had somehow appeared magically there.

These men got up in the middle of the night, worked through hard labour with fervour and camaraderie, all to feed their families, and for essentially very little by way of financial reward. Maybe enough to get by, she imagined, after keeping the boat maintained and full of fuel, and all the safety precautions, not so much for legalities but to keep each other as safe as they could when roughing the high seas.

Sitting silently watching them work, Sasha was gaining a new appreciation of the way these men worked. Men of the earth, or sea, working a real, proper job. In truth, she realised she might have more respect for the baggage handlers when she finally got back to the airport.

More than that appreciation, however, was the concentration on how much she was watching Col more than the others…. She wondered how she hadn't noticed he had somehow relieved himself of the thick jumper he had been wearing when she got there, and was now exposing a pair of rather impressive biceps, in a dirty white vest that stood out in the low pre-dawn light.

Whether the hard work had been getting to him, or whether he'd simply spilled something on his sweater she had missed, but becoming increasingly aware that his frame was not at all hideous to the eye, she failed to realise how much more time she was spending gazing dreamily at him, as opposed to taking in the whole scene.

Col had in fact been getting warm from doing most of the manual work, partly out of deference to the older men and partly to work off some of his frustrations. Despite it being the early hours of the morning in March, he was really feeling a little overheated.

For his part, he was wondering to himself if Sasha's proximity had anything to do with the heat suddenly increasing since her arrival. The beard wasn't helping either. Even after 3 years of growing the disguise, he still wasn't too comfortable with it. He didn't really have too much time to worry about how much of a show he would be putting on if he removed a layer. In all honesty, he had actually forgotten he had a sleeveless vest on underneath the sweater and not a regular t-shirt.

He had purposefully decided not to glance in Sasha's direction, and had succeeded until, just as the sky was getting lighter, Derek smirked and noticed her dreamy gaze, cocking his head in her direction to notify his crewmate. Col made the mistake of looking. The dawn light was just enough to display her face with a soft glow, light shining in her eyes, her hair loose around her shoulders as she had left it down to account for the cool night air. Their glances crossed and she blushed and looked away. "Right, ready for the away then Cap'n!" called Steve. "Fresh crab for yer lunch when we get back missy" grinned the Captain as he cocked his cap to her.

She smiled a thank you and marvelled as Col pulled himself aboard, before slipping his sweater back over his torso.

"What time?" She called, to no one in particular. Col looked out to sea, turned back to her and said, "Never really sure what time, but how's about we say 10-ish?"

She couldn't be sure, but delaying her answer as she tried to read his expression, she could have sworn it was intended as an invitation to something more than handing over leftovers.

“I’ll be here waiting.” She smiled, genuinely excited. This time, there was no mistaking the wink from the Captain directed to her as he stood behind Col. Col, oblivious to the captain’s interference, nodded a parting to her, and turned away to concentrate on what he needed to. Sasha held back to watch as the vessel disappeared around the head to the open sea.

At 10am she returned, never expecting the boat to be anywhere near on time, but to her amazement she saw them approaching Tregiffen as she walked down the hill. Ol’George looked over the moon to see her and handed her a bag.

“Special order for the young lady. Give ‘em to Martha she’ll know what ter do – special fish supper for you tonight.”

“Thank you!” Sasha beamed with a slight giggle of surprise.

When she glanced in the bag, however, she was a little disconcerted when she saw whole un-filleted fish and crabs – thankful for the advice to hand the whole thing over the Martha. She glanced up and noticed Col, recently come up from below deck, not hiding an amused smile at her reaction.

Sasha bit her bottom lip in insecurity. Not sure what to say next, she nodded politely, and hiked back up the hill to the ‘Rest’ where she found Martha where she left her, polishing the brass door plate to Royal standards.

“Ooh, dinner, eh?” Martha raised her eyebrows “I know just what’ll go nice with that!”

“George ‘as taken a likin to you it seems, Sasha.” Jimmy said as she entered the pub. He was ticking stock off a list, checking his inventory behind the bar, counting bottles. He barely looked up when she came through the door, seemingly instinctively to know it was her.

“I know. Not sure why!” She answered “Barely knows anything about me”

Martha and Jimmy exchanged a knowing glance, that Sasha was fully aware of.

“What?” She enquired, looking between the two.

“You know how the Cap’n can get over ‘is crew….” said Martha “We don’t get many newcomers down ‘ere – they all heads fer Sennen or Penzance. Lucky if they get anyone younger ‘n fifty buying anything but holiday homes in St Buryan any more” Jimmy continued, by way of an in depth explanation which was still going over Sasha’s head. Sasha raised her eyebrows and stared at Martha.

Martha read her confused expression.

“Sasha, it would seem that George has got it into his head that his lad Colan down there needs some help in finding some companionship. Don’t think he’s mentioned it to Col either but ‘e don’t seem to be sparing any opportunity to leave the two of you young'uns together"

Before Sasha had any kind of chance to express an opinion about the revelation, the door swung open and Colan fell through it.

The awkward silence didn't seem enough to tell him he was being spoken about before his arrival, as much as giving him the impression his tumbling entrance was what had surprised them all.

"Sorry, Martha"

Sasha could have sworn for that split second, two words, his Cornish accent disappeared and he seemed more like a reprimanded public schoolboy.

"Um…the door was open – had expected it to be locked, see, was gonna lean on it for a sec before….." Col's voice trailed off as though his excuse had run out of steam.

Neither Martha nor Jimmy moved an inch. Sasha felt heat rising in her face and looked away to avoid giving any impression of embarrassment that would cause him to query.

"I was….erm…." Colan for the first time since Sasha's arrival seemed unsure of himself.

Not confident, cocky, bullish and rough as she had been seeing him so far. He was in the presence of these two, village elders she supposed, to his status as a "newcomer" quite polite, and respectful of his elders.

For a moment Sasha forgot her embarrassment and became, once again, intrigued with the man. Martha knowingly nodded and decided to help him along a little.

"It would seem, being as you're free for the rest of the day that Sasha may be at a loose end until dinner this evening. I'm not sure she's been up to Land's End yet, eh Sasha?" Martha looked at her, her eyebrows raised out of Col's line of sight, indication that some affirmation of her statement may assist.

Sasha, almost speechless, managed a nod and an "mmm" noise, before Col caught on to Martha's suggestion and continued.

"Oh, well, I do have a crate of fresh crabs to take up to the hotel then I'm free, if you needed a ride anywhere." Colan looked directly at Sasha, without a hint of disdain, sarcasm, condescension. Just pure hope. Sasha felt her cheeks burning up.

7

Knowing full well she was backed into a corner, Sasha had no choice. The glaringly obvious had been stated to her by her jovial hosts; if she so obviously rebuffed him, and Ol'George's attempts now, she may as well have punched them all in the face and kissed the rest of her week in Cornwall goodbye.

"That'd be great. Thanks" She lowered her head to avoid everyone's glances and pushed past Col, out through the heavy door. Outside he followed her to the truck waiting at the curb.

They were silent as Col reached past her easily to open the door for her in a gentlemanly fashion.

Sasha nodded a silent thank you without looking up at him.

Col went round to the driver side.

"You didn't have to." She told him after they'd both climbed into the cab.

"Kinda why I came in. Cap'n had suggested much the same thing. Old people round 'ere seem to be in the same frame of mind all the time."

"I noticed" Sasha smiled at the thought of the whole village thinking in unison. Col looked at her smile and felt the awkwardness of the initial moment suddenly melt away, and smiled a silent laugh in return. He started the engine and they chugged their way up the hill and out of the village. Sasha watched the countryside pass, and something in the fresh air blowing on her face from the sea through the open window, gave her confidence to broach the subject they'd been avoiding.

"So it would seem that Ol'George has got it into his head……" She began.

"I got the impression they're trying a bit of match….." he spoke at the same time.

"…Making?" continued Sasha.

Col seemed to be blushing, she thought, although it was practically impossible to tell through that mop of hair on his face.

"Sorry." He mumbled.

"It's ok." Sasha told him, matter-of-factly.

"It's just, they're not used to bachelors, down 'ere, in this environment" he continued, apologetically.

"I don't suppose they have much else by way of excitement to fill their time." Sasha offered.

"There is that," he mused, with a slight scoff.

"Look, I'll be gone on Sunday anyway, so it can all go

back to normal."

"Yeah, right. 'Course." Col shrugged.

Silence befell them again, as though that were the end of it.

Each unbeknownst to the other, however, were trying to think of some way of continuing the line of conversation. After silence for a full 5 minutes, which seemed infinitely longer in silence, Sasha opted for small talk.

"So did your meeting go well?" She realised almost as soon as she said it, he took that as not so much small talk but a full on interrogation.

"Meeting? I said that was nothing!" And so silence befell them once again.

"Maybe we should start again? Conversing, I mean, by way of an introduction? I mean…"Sasha took a deep breath and turned to him, holding out a hand, at which he glanced sideways briefly between watching the road.

"My name is Sasha Pender. I am 29. I work at an airport in Passenger services."

Col carried on driving for a few moments, looking between her outstretched hand and her face. Turning back to the road, he pulled into a siding near a large caravan park, opposite a large, imposing pub called "The Wreckers".

Satisfying himself the truck as stopped and off the road,

he turned back and took her hand. "Colan Tangye. Col. From up the coast. Came down here 3 years ago looking for somethin' new. Me old boat and crew disbanded – went out o' business. Only thing I ever knew, fishin', after me dad. " He cursed himself inside for sounding far too well rehearsed. Thankfully, Sasha hadn't seemed to have noticed.

"OK." Sasha took a deep breath. He nodded, started the engine again and headed off again towards Land's End.

"You know," she began again, "when I first saw you on the boat, fully dressed up in your fishing gear, head down, long beard, thought you were much older."

Col suddenly recognised why some of her initial reaction to him, then, had seemed that of revulsion. What 29 year old wanted the kind of kissing comments he'd suggested at their first meeting from some salty old sea dog old enough to be her grandfather. Sasha tried to back pedal a little.

"Only until I actually saw your face, of course, then you seemed a bit younger....maybe....." Sasha faltered off, as though bringing the subject of age was a little rude.

"I'm 38. If it mattered to anything."

"Just interesting to know." Sasha smiled at him, and he, unexpectedly and quite comfortably, smiled back.

They pulled in to the car park at the tourist-aimed complex that adorned the area at the very end of the A30; commonly known as the end of the UK.

"You have to admit, " Sasha pointed out, as she stood near him while he unloaded the crate to be delivered to the hotel's restaurant, "It must seem a little strange to them, to a lot of people, someone like you, fit, in your prime, single? No interested parties?"

"Fit, eh?" his eyes twinkled with knowing excitement, as much as he tried to hide it. Sasha blushed.

"Oh…just playing devil's advocate"

"It's a long story."

"It's ok. I mean, if you're batting for the other side…working on a boat...it may be best…"

"I'm not gay!" he all but shouted at her; attracting the attention of a family passing from their car to the gift shop complex. He lowered his head and nodded in their direction. "Like I said, long story."

Sasha took a cue to remain silent for the moment. She followed him along the paved walkways he knew so well, but a step back, partly to muse at the gift shops and tourist-ware in the shops lining the courtyard style cobblestones that led up to the main hotel and restaurant, partly to allow Col time to cool off.

She had stopped to read a wall plaque about smugglers and pirates for which Cornwall was famous from the old days when he returned from dropping off his wares.

"All done?" Col smiled apologetically. "Walk? There's a garden over here."

Sasha nodded, and followed his lead as he walked away from the main whitewashed group of buildings. She saw a path that went off, signposted that it led to a miniature farm style petting zoo, but Col walked straight ahead, and stopped at a small patch or flowers and bright green, well-watered grass.

“It’s a memorial. To four boys who got into trouble on the cliffs and died around here.” He explained as she looked at the sign naming the spot.

“There used to be a cottage on this spot with a water well outside it.” Col continued, “My grandmother used to live in it for a while. Before Land’s End was sold to the developers and built up as it is today. Used to pretty much be a car park back then, when that signpost up on the point was new, a novelty when cameras were becoming common use, and people would travel John O’Groats to Land’s End as a challenge. They still do, charity bike rides and the like. There’s another sign post at the top end.”

“Wow. John O’Groats is Scotland, right?”

“Yeah. “ He paused and looked out to sea. A perfectly calm and clear day, the lighthouse on Carn Bras perfectly in view. “That there is Longships lighthouse.”

Sasha was becoming increasingly enthralled at being shown around by this imposing man who the more time she spent with him, appeared more and more passionate and intelligent than she would ever have initially given him credit for.

Leigh always did warn her she was a snob, and never to judge a book by its cover. Sasha had always tried to contradict her but something told her Leigh knew her better than she knew herself.

Without planning anything, Col led her on a hike around the edge of the cliffs, pointing out the names of various landmarks along the way. They headed towards a rope bridge that she was surprised to see there, and then up on to a rock, Col held out his hand.

“Here,” he held her hand with a strength offering the most amazing feeling of safety and security she had ever imagined. “Look there, down there in the rocks” He pointed, pulling her closer to him so she could feel his breath on the nape of her neck, in order that she follow the same line of sight as him. To her surprise she saw a shipwreck. “Wow!” she breathed “A real shipwreck? I thought they were all from days gone by!”

Col looked down his chest to where her other hand lay, steadying herself. He savoured the moment, allowing himself to believe for one second he could let her get close.

“This one’s Mulheim. Ran aground in 2003” He moved, to indicate they should step down, and, more importantly, move apart.

Sasha, moving, realised where her hand was for the first time, and froze, staring into his face, trying to read some kind of reaction. Simultaneously she realised she was consciously noting how firm his chest felt, even through the vest she knew he was wearing and the sweater he still wore over it. She moved back and started to led the way back up the path.

"So there are still accidents and shipwrecks these days? With all the modern technology and things learned?"

"The sea will always be a very dangerous place. We can learn all we can learn but there will still be dangers, unknowns, variables, that we can never master."

Sasha was impressed by his sudden outburst of wisdom; and once again knew there was far more to Col than she had given him credit for. He caught her eye and motioned they continue waking back up to the restaurant.

They sat outside the bar on the cliffs with drinks Colan treated them to. Neither wanted to leave yet, Sasha was enjoying his company and wanted to experience a bit more; trying not to pry with probing questions that she knew he wouldn't answer and would make him clam up even more.

Col told himself that just talking would be no harm to her. Learn more about her to fulfil his need to know about another person to see him through the rest of his time here. Don't touch a hair on her head, give her no reason to stay, she would go on Sunday and return to her life.

So he led the conversation, asking about her life, the airport, her friends, and the people she saw on a daily basis. He learned about her without her realising – No father at all – and she'd never pushed her mother for any information. An older brother, great uncle, not much of an extended family at all. Mother's brother had moved away with his children, her cousins.

Her tales of her friends at work were amusing enough to allow her to carry on talking as he gazed to memorise enough of her to dream of, the cute curve of her nose, how her hair glistened in the sun reflecting back up at them from the Atlantic, her strong but not masculine calf muscles and dainty ankles, he imagined in pert courtly high heels tottering around the airport, amusing himself with the image of her ordering unsuspecting passengers around in her….what colour had she said? Uniform… Before they knew it, the sun was setting.

"You should write these stories down." He told her, over their fourth coffee and smiling at the most recent anecdote. Sasha simply shook her head and laughed, as though he was joking.

"I really should get back, I think. Martha was really excited about dinner this evening. I don't think she'll let me forget it if I miss it." Col agreed and they climbed into the truck to head back. Their journey home, having been talked out, was once again silent.

But this time, having broken through a little of the tension, having talked and talked about, really, Sasha thought, virtually nothing of any value, all day, their silence was comfortable.

Sasha climbed down from the cab as Col stopped outside

the Inn. She half expected him to join her, and come in for some food, but he kept the engine running. She turned to thank him before closing the door.

"No problem. " She moved to close the passenger door behind her, but he leaned over and pushed it open again, almost knocking her in the nose.

"God, sorry" he said, an alarmed expression covering his face "are you OK?" She smiled and nodded. "I was going to mention, the fish festival begins up at Newlyn tomorrow and it's my day off. Not as fishy as it sounds other stuff, just there's stalls, crafts, food, music , dancing…." He continued.

"No that sounds good. I'd love to" she beamed at him. He looked a little taken aback, "Oh, I mean, if that's what you meant?" Sasha suddenly realised she may have assumed an invitation when there wasn't one…

"Yeah, yeah. Did you want to go?" Col's eyes seemed more pleadingly desperate than she could ever have imagined they would.

"What time?"

"Say 9.30?"

"No problem." She smiled, stepped back and closed the door. As she was left wondering that his accent seemed to have dropped away again, he waved, nodded and drove away. Sasha stopped a moment, wondering what she was doing, and entered the pub.

Jimmy was behind the bar, wiping a glass to within an inch of its life. Two men sat in the back corner of the pub deep in conversation about something quietly. Derek sat at the bar and raised his glass to her as she smiled at him.

Martha stood in the doorway leading through to the kitchen and the accommodations upstairs. She glanced over Sasha's shoulder inquisitively, as though checking to see if Col was joining them.

"He…seemed like he had to go." Sasha felt the need, for some reason, to apologise for his absence. She wasn't his keeper…far from it…although it seemed at times that he seemed protection from these villagers.

Sasha ate well and laughed with Martha that evening while Jimmy tended bar. Sasha did her best to keep the conversation away from any mention or probing on her relationship or lack of with Col. She managed to keep Martha on a steady stream of the old days, how she met Jimmy, what it was like in the 70's when the Skewjack surf village was popular and a regular parade of hot young free things would parade through the area in the summers.

Sasha couldn't sleep immediately when she retired that evening. She sat on the window seat with the window open and listened to the sounds of the sea.

She realised she was getting very, very, scared that the more time she spent with Col Tangye, the more he was penetrating her soul – physically she already knew the way she felt when he was near – which seemed to be getting nearer, and more often – meant she would have trouble resisting if close became very close. She knew, somehow, if she did allow that to happen, then she'd be left with the problem of not being able to forget him; as she had many others before him.

She lay on her bed and allowed herself to drift off to sleep; knowing full well that the man she dreamed about more often than not, now, had taken on fully the physical form, and face, of Col Tangye, without the beard he seemed to be hiding behind. She awoke the next morning feeling as though she had been made love to a million times by a man she knew for some reason, she shouldn't.

8

After a cold shower, Sasha dressed and checked in the mirror she looked as conservative, in the least possible way attractive while remaining presentable, as possible. Plain white t-shirt and a casual waistcoat and black jeans, seemed appropriately casual and comfortable. She hadn't wanted to appear rude as to turn down Col's invitation, at very least so she could please Martha by telling her Col was taking her out.

Besides, she wanted to experience the festival and a bit more of Cornwall's culture. He was there dead on 9.30am, as promised. He was nothing if not punctual. Odd, for someone from such a sleepy place, whose job depended on how the fishing was that day and the tides, as opposed to military timing.

They drove to Newlyn, about half an hour back up the South coast towards Penzance. The town was buzzing with all kinds. An international contingent of Canadian fishermen and Breton Fishermen were in attendance, showing solidarity to their fellow seamen, and sharing wares and tales and tips and tricks.

There was live music playing constantly, folk bands; wannabe rock stars from around the county; "The

Fisherman's Friends" singing sea shanties and solo guitarists singing ballads making the hardened fish wives melt and wonder what would life be like if they had married a singer instead of a good solid working-man who got his hands dirty, assumed you never needed to be told you looked beautiful and expected their meal on the table at supper time.

There were increasing numbers of "gourmet" food vans appearing – none of your bog standard cockles and mussels, and fish and chips – these were celebrity chefs with their own seafood restaurants charging rich Londoners four times as much for half a plateful, because it had a sprig of parsley on it, charging £10 for a plate of samples to the festival goers.

Sasha and Col seemed to forget about the expectations they had placed on them by their elders down the coast; or what they had been each trying to avoid, and simply enjoy themselves.

Col introduced some of the locals that he had come to know to Sasha. She tried some fresh tuna he held out for her on a plastic fork. Huge chunks of fresh tuna steak, not the washed out tinned flakes she'd grown up on, and was amazed.

They washed it down with some samples of traditional Cornish Cider from a local "scrumpy" farm.

As the alcohol loosened them both ever so slightly, they had a go at some of the carnival stalls, coconut shies and shooting galleries that lit up as darkness fell – before they had even realised they had been there so long.

By the time the bigger live bands began to appear on the main stage, Sasha and Col had allowed themselves to be side-tracked so much and been sampling various ciders that when they ordered what must have been their seventh drink from the bar, and found empty chairs to sit on, they were both as relaxed as either of them had been for a very long time.

Sasha found herself feeling a little down, and in her slightly inebriated state, was unable to disguise the melancholy look on her face. Col, equally unguarded, became concerned.

"You OK?"

"I've only got a couple of days left." She turned her gaze away from the stage and looked directly into his eyes; all inhibitions drowned in cider.

"It's been so long since I had a holiday, got away, on my own and allowed myself to relax…"

"Not looking forward to going back?" Col enquired.

"It's just…everything's been so…tense…." She shrugged. "Just since September…the plane crashes. I mean, we weren't affected directly, we didn't send a plane there or know anyone on them. One of our girls moved to New York a couple of years ago but her mum let us know that she was fine, she'd been out of town."

"But?"

"It's strange....it's like a ripple effect that's changing everything...I have a strange feeling, like we're not going to survive. Like it's suddenly all going to go downhill....So many airlines are struggling – it's got to have some effect. Everyone who comes through now are all on edge and not really seeming as carefree as they used to be – and then they get extra frisking and extra searches and not as much freedom at security..."

"Sasha..."

"nah....don't mind me.....it's the cider talkin' I think" She grinned – putting on a Cornish Accent.

Col grinned back at her, relaxed; comforted she'd pulled herself back up again. He would have hated to see her end their day miserable. A four-piece folk band struck up a set and the mood livened up immediately. Random people got up and started dancing. For once, Col swallowed his fears and his pride and told himself one night of fun wasn't harming anyone. It seemed like everyone was here anyway. They were hardly alone.

"Ms Pender, would ya care t'dance?" He stood, held out his hand to her and pulled her from her perch. She laughed uncontrollably but fell into a natural rhythm as he led her round the courtyard-come-dance floor. They must've been dancing for two or three number nonstop before Col realised he was holding her closer and closer each time, and the track changed to a slower tempo and she was pressed up against him, her head leaning on his chest. He closed his eyes and bent his head down to kiss the top of her head, then resting his cheek sideways on her head, taking in the scent of her hair. She seemed to revel in the closeness as her body started to respond in instinctive ways. She pressed closer to him, moving her arms down his back towards the seat of his jeans and slid her hands in her back pockets.

A sudden revelation hit them both at the same time as to what was occurring, her head snapped up to stare deep into his eyes as he swallowed hard and stared back at her. There seemed no other logical move than to bend down and take her lips in his. The sensation of her lips meeting his created sparks to his very core that made him wonder if he could stop this now he had broken the invisible seal that was holding these feelings in. Sasha's eyes closed as she allowed this to happen to her.

Something made her unable and totally unwilling to fight back. His strong arms enveloped her completely and she felt like he could almost lift her up completely, effortlessly. Although she'd never kissed a man with a beard before, she seemed to not even notice it was there. She realised this sensation drifting through her to her core was exactly the same, if not better, than she had been dreaming about. And then a vibration from his pocket snapped his attention away. He stopped suddenly, as though pained; his hand drew straight to his pocket and pulled out his mobile. He dragged his troubled gaze away from her saddened eyes and stared at the screen.

"I'm sorry…." He murmured "I have to….." He rushed away and answered the phone, turning his back to her and disappearing behind the beer tent.

Sasha stood in a moment of frozen panic. She recovered her composure, looked around for a moment to check she hadn't been made a complete fool of.

OK not many people were looking at her. She might recover. Short of chasing after him like an abandoned puppy, her pride stepped in. Right then, she decided, I shall take this opportunity to go to the ladies.

She slowly and carefully recovered the use of her legs and wandered coolly to the portable toilets on the far side of the stage. After relieving a few pints of cider she felt a little more alive, a little less affected by the alcohol.

What HAD she been thinking? Crazy! Exiting the booth, she heard Col's voice. Realising the other end of the toilet block came out behind the same beer tent he had ducked behind; she headed in his direction to get an explanation and to be taken home.

She started walking with a purpose but as she neared his location, she became aware that his tone had taken on the dangerous, warning level again. This time, he was using it on someone else.

And his accent had changed yet again, almost a Scottish twinge to it "Yeah everyone else is busy but the tides are all wrong. You go ahead with it tonight pal, and I'm gonna turn you in myself or else kill ya.... ... I don't give a crap Juan – you stick to the original drop or I'll end this me sel'. There is no conspiracy yer dreamin. If there were I'd be the first one to change it"

He snapped the flip-phone shut and turned, staring straight into Sasha's stunned face.

"Fuck you scared the crap outta me!"

There. Definitely not Cornish. A definite Scottish twang mixed with public schoolboy who spent too long in London's east end? God what the hell is going on with him?

Sasha turned on her heels and ran, not sure where but towards noise, yes, people. Safety in numbers. And maybe the cider was still affecting her more than she thought. She felt as though she was having trouble breathing.

I just need to think. Sasha stood alone, on the edge of the dance floor, her mind spinning so much that thinking was nigh on impossible. She felt a hand cover hers. She knew whose it was, she just couldn't look up. After a pause, she wondered to herself why he was holding it so gently, carefully. What had she been imagining, that he would chase her down, grab her roughly and drag her away?

Yes, she told herself, that's exactly what I was thinking…

"Sash," She still dared not move. "Sasha." She turned to look questioningly at him. His eyes were soft, not threatening, more worried, concerned that she had changed her opinion of him, "Let's go and talk."

Col knew he shouldn't be driving – if they'd been caught

there was no way he could have explained being so far over the limit. He sped along the deserted country lanes and didn't stop until he reached the end of the road and the car park at Land's End.

Without a glance in her direction, he climbed out of the driver's seat. Before she knew it he was at her door, holding it open for her. Still, without looking at her, he grabbed her hand and pulled her from the vehicle, holding her hand so tightly as though he never wanted to let her go. With his free hand he slammed the door, and led her purposefully away from the direction of the hotel, to an almost deserted part of the landscape.

Sasha found she was having trouble keeping up with him. He was so much taller than her, longer legs and a bigger stride; she was taking two steps to each of his single bounds. He drew her round to face him and sat her down, as though she were a child, on a rock behind her, and for the first time, looked into her face.

As though realising her was standing too tall for any meaningful dialogue to take place, he shook his head and sat down beside her, lowering himself almost to her level.

Col turned his torso to face her, Sasha remained facing out to sea, scared to look into his face.

"I told myself to stay away and now I've broken that promise and I can't change what's happened but you need to know…"Col started "I don't want to hurt you."

"Who are you?" Sasha pressed

“Someone trying to help…”

“Help? Help who?”

“I…” he shook his head “…I shouldn’t say”

“Why the hell not? I mean really, I’ve been here a few days and it’s really none of my business regardless of what’s been going on in my own head, but even I don’t want anyone to be hurting George and Ned and Derek and Steve or anyone else in….”

“In your head?” Col cut over her. He had suddenly forgotten about trying to explain himself. His demeanour changed from dark despair crossed with chastised schoolboy, to suddenly very, very, interested to know what she was thinking.

Sasha froze and realised what she’d said. Maybe it was the alcohol in her system, maybe the heady rush she was still under from the memory of his lips tasting hers and the feel of his hands on her body or maybe the way he was looking at her, the stress she had sensed from him ebbed away and his eyes glistened with fascination and anticipation as she looked into them.

“I…I’ve been having…dreams. Graphic…really…graphic…sexual…dreams...for quite some time. “

“Graphic? “ Col smirked at her. Sasha raised her eyebrows accusingly

“Sorry…”

“You get the picture. I just, for some reason, this week, the person in the dreams has kind of…started to….lookabitlikeyou” She rushed the last part of the sentence out in case she chickened out before it came out.

Col was silent for what seemed like an age.

“Really?”

“Look it’s not like I mean to dream them or seem to have any control over what I dream about, ” She looked at him sheepishly. “It’s just that, these dreams leave me waking up feeling…a little…kind of like it wasn’t a dream at all…”

“Wow” breathed Col. Wow, he thought, how’s that for sexual frustration?

“Yeah” Sasha heaved a sigh of relief. He’s taking this better than I thought.

“So, what kind of things did you…or We…get up to in these dreams to make you feel like this?” Sasha stared at him, shocked.

“Well,” he continued, producing a hip flask from his pocket, swigging some and offering her some. She glanced between him and the flask questioningly.

“Dutch courage?” He explained. She grabbed it and gulped a large quantity. Sasha gulped,

“It’s like drinking nail varnish remover”

Col smiled, replaced the cap and put the flask back in his back pocket. He removed his sweater, folder it neatly and placed it on the ground behind her carefully.

“I wish I hadn’t told you.” Sasha apologised.

“Do you?” he asked, reaching under her chin with an index finger and turning her head to face him.

Sasha at the mere thought of these dreams in his presence could feel her heart begin to pound; a twitching sensation between her legs warned her any more contact from him was going to send her spiralling out of control.

Oh God he’s taken his jumper off, she finally noticed, look at those arms…

Col stopped her heavy breathing placing his mouth over hers once again, hungrily probing her mouth with his tongue. God he’s good, she mused, allowing herself to encircle his neck with her arms. Somehow, she’d forgotten about the fear that had stemmed from overhearing his phone call.

With a mixture of shock and delight she suddenly realized he was far more similar to the man in her dreams than she had first thought, he felt exactly the same as she had dreamed of.

“So?“ he muttered into her hair, “these dreams?”

“Here” was about all she could manage, running a finger loosely down her neck, and he traced the line with his tongue.

“Here” she continued tracing her finger down her chest, between her breasts over her loose t-shirt. Col put a strong arm around her middle and slowly lowered her back onto the soft springy grass behind her, her head resting perfectly on the sweater he had deftly and perfectly placed there previously.

Sasha knew she couldn’t fight it if she tried. Shifting to ensure total possible comfort, the thrill of getting this close to Col and out in the open air was too strong to fight.

She grabbed his hand and pushed it down her leg, then clasping her own smaller hand over his, guided it up her thigh and forwards, so his hand was resting over below the zip of her jeans.

“Hey, control freak” he muttered into her neck, through kisses,

“Living through the dream” she whispered, eyes closed, “you’re definitely him” she confirmed, mostly to herself.

This is the man I’ve been dreaming of. Col lifted himself up on his left elbow, hand holding himself up looking down over her. The darkness in this near-wilderness was adding to the eroticism of the experience – he wondered if they could get away with doing away with clothes all together.

Col slowly and gently began to tug at the bottom of her t-shirt and guide it up her torso. Sasha joined him and lifted herself enough for him to be able to get it over her head. As her top moved up her face and she pulled it off the remaining distance his mouth immediately took hers again, as his hand moved down to start on her jeans.

Sasha was fully aware that the anticipation all afternoon and the intensity of the passion she had been experiencing since the dancing at Newlyn had ensured the dampness between her thighs was unmistakable, soaking through her underwear and jeans – there was no way she would be able to hide her almost involuntary excitement from him.

In the darkness, Col felt a thrill shiver through him at the realisation at how wet she had become purely from wanting him. How could this be wrong when they both obviously needed each other so much? Sasha pushed him off and rolled over. She stood up. “Sorry, can’t wait”. She kicked off her shoes, glancing around pulled off her jeans. Col recovered his initial shock and suddenly joined her to do the same.

9

Sasha was in two minds about her underwear. Standing there with the night air surrounding her bare legs, and able to make out his frame against darkness, she said "sod it", removed her knickers, then lunged forward to grab his face in her hands and kiss him again.

Without breaking their kiss, Col did the same with his boxers, and wrapped his strong arms around her, lifting her effortlessly.

"Oh my goodness" she gasped breaking away from his mouth and throwing her arms around his neck, and her legs around his waist in terror.

The terror subsided into a shiver. Col grinned as he felt her nakedness against his. Sasha became aware of his erection; although where she was gripping around his middle with her thighs it was slightly below her vulva. She leaned in again to kiss him hungrily as he realized her hips were beginning to gyrate – as far as he could tell, involuntarily, he wondered if she was aware of it.

Col turned to lower her back to the ground again, perfectly aiming for the same location she had been previously with the sweater for a pillow. She was surrounded by the scent of him, his hair, his clothes, and the musky, surprisingly animal attractiveness of his musky perspiration, and not a trace of the stronger scents from the fishing boat.

If she hadn't known better or thought it too odd to be present Sasha could have sworn she noticed the smell of fresh dry cleaning mixed in too – although in her present state of euphoria that could have been part of the recurring dream that was quickly becoming reality so that she couldn't tell the difference between the two.

Col could wait no longer and was in no state or mood to be careful; with one quick move he entered her.

Ooh there it is, thought Sasha in her euphoria, that's what I've been imagining all these nights…except….better…Far better…

For what seemed like an age, neither of them moved. Sasha was filled with joy and relief at the pure feeling of him inside her, the size of him and the blood pumping through his erection creating an unimaginably exhilarating feeling to surge through her. Col had stalled with a combination of similar feelings of relief and pleasure at her hot, soft and welcoming core, combined with the sudden realisation of what he'd just done. Before he could dwell on the thought, a soft moan escaped Sasha's lips which pushed him over the edge – there was no way he could stop now. Col began to move in a rhythm she matched. In his fever and desperation he felt it would have been so easy to go thundering ahead like a bull in a china shop but aware of their public location and a hotel nearby, and Sasha's gentle, but purposeful movements keeping him in check, Col relaxed his breathing a little and continued in perfect rhythm, falling forward to kiss her deeply while still managing to keep them both building towards the most erotic moment of each of their lives.

Col knew there could no longer be any holding back and allowed his orgasm to take over him, and his semen shot into her.

Sasha, feeling him reach his peak and his fluid shooting into her body, which reacted with her own orgasm shuddering through her, holding in the scream she wanted to exhale and biting her bottom lip with a protracted moan, so hard she felt her lip begin to bleed. Col collapsed on top of her, however constantly aware of not crushing her still managing to hold himself up slightly to one side, their legs entwining in comfort and his head lying on the grass bending down over hers protectively. Sasha shifted her position so she could rest her head on his chest.

Col smiled with satisfaction, raised one arm above his head and lay it on the grass and moved the sweater to behind his head. He stared up at the stars and toyed with her hair falling around his fingers as he stroked her head. Sasha felt almost hypnotised by the comforting rising and falling of his chest, and the feel of his bicep under her neck. Neither of them wanted to move. Moments turned into seconds turned in to minutes, and finally, Col noticed the sky was ever so faintly lightening.

“Shit.” He spluttered, rousing Sasha from her dreamlike state “What time is it?”

“Oh God, already?” she exclaimed. They dressed quickly without one more word, and hurried to the truck. Making their way back to Tregiffen was silent, urgent and uncomfortable. Sasha kept glancing sideways, wanting so much to reach out and just hold on to his arm; never let go and be near him forever now she had found him.

Col felt as though his world was about to come crashing down around him. Everything he’d built up around him relied on not letting anyone get close enough to distract him; or get into danger themselves.

He stopped outside the ‘Rest’ and waited for her to get out. Just as her hand reached for the door handle, he turned and grabbed her face and kissed her deeply once more, breathing in the scent of her and trying to record the feel of her skin in his hands.

The longing for the night to have lasted forever was clear in each other’s eyes as they both held the stare for as long as they could, before Col could no longer ignore the motions down at the Quay as “Claudia” prepared to launch. Sasha blushed and dropped his gaze, turned and hurried inside.

It was Saturday morning. Sasha sneaked up to her room and stared at herself in the mirror. Did that really happen or was that another one of those dreams? Replaying the events of the previous 24 hours in her head, she suddenly felt scared.

The sex was…oh the sex had been so amazing, exactly as she had imagined, as she had been dreaming about; the time spent with Colan when they weren't trying to hide anything, comfortable in his company, eating and drinking and dancing in a carefree world. But his dark side scared her. He could turn so dramatically into a shady character that chilled her to her core.

He could silence her with a mere stare and she knew from his activities and the overheard phone call, there was something more going on with him than him being a simple crewman on a fishing boat.

At best, what if he was bi-polar or simply quick-tempered enough to turn on someone and become violent? Sasha sat on the window seat, and watched the early morning sunbeams dancing on the ocean through the window. Before long, the boat would return.

How uncomfortable is the next meeting going to be? She wondered. It seemed harsh, but her train ticket was for tomorrow. She would be back at work on Monday morning at 4am.

If she left now, made a clean break, got back to her own life and left him to his as he had originally seemed to desire, they would both move on with their lives and become nothing but a distant memory of a wonderful night in the outdoors… Or am I just running away from change and all the challenges it might bring, like I always do? She asked herself, as she began packing her things, and checking her phone for train times.

It was only an hour later by the time she reached the station at Penzance. Sasha saw the next train heading for Bristol Temple Meads sitting on the platform as she jumped from the bus. She ran into the ticket office and managed to alter her Sunday ticket for today and board the train just before the guard's whistle blew.

If she'd timed it right she'd only have to wait about half an hour in Bristol for her connecting train. She'd left a note with Martha to give to Colan. She'd told Martha the envelope just contained a ten pound note in payment for the food and drink he'd purchased the day before; she'd left her purse and promised to pay him back. Martha nodded and smiled. She explained to Martha she had an early shift on Monday and had decided a day at home on Sunday to get her uniform ready and finish her laundry would be more relaxing than rushing after getting off an afternoon train. She settled back on the train as it pulled from the station.

It was relatively quiet, so she had the seat to herself and the one opposite wasn't occupied either, so she felt like she had a little privacy. She could have spent the journey going over and over her time in Cornwall but having not slept since leaving for the fish festival the day before she really didn't have the energy to concentrate. Sasha slept most of the way to Bristol. It was the first time in months any sleep had not been interrupted by the recurring dream. Maybe, just maybe, she had managed to get it out of her system, finally.

Oblivious to Sasha's departure, "Claudia" glided back into the harbour effortlessly. Such calm waters Ol'George hadn't seen in a long time. He was a little glad, since he'd been aware of Colan's tardiness that morning and wondered about his state of mind. In one way, the lad had been more attentive, alert and physically lithe than he'd seemed in a long time on that morning's expedition; but on the other, in the restful moments he seemed distracted and listless.

As soon as they docked and Colan was free to leave, George having told him Derek and Ned could take the catch again today for a little more practice. The Captain watched him almost skip up the hill towards the 'Rest'. Just as I thought – something to do with the girl, he smiled to himself, after Martha had been gossiping about them heading off to Newlyn yesterday.

"Is Sasha upstairs?" Col enquired of Martha at the door of the pub as she swept the front step.

"Oh you'll be wanting the envelope she left then?" Martha gave him a concerned look, trying to read his expression.

"Left?"

"She decided to change her train back, I did wonder if she'd told you, working early on Monday apparently."

Without a word, Col stormed out; Martha watching him go, sadly.

10

Sasha was intent on distracting herself.

She spent all Sunday morning rushing round her home, cleaning and tidying anything and everything to within an inch of its life. She spent a meticulous two hours ensuring her uniform was properly cleaned and pressed and hung on the hanger ready for the next morning.

She played housework pop music at full blast to push the physical feeling of euphoria from the image of one man she'd never have again from reaching a peak.

Inadvertently, her mind wandered to work. And then it wandered past the actual work and to conversations and discussions they would have in the staff room in between actually working. And the Cosmo articles and finally…on to sex and positions and the differences between men and women...And her mind's eye started picturing Col again… and she knew it was time to take a break.

She perched on the edge of her sofa, sipping cold water to cool off from the sweat she'd worked up, partly from the frenzied cleaning, partly from the overactive imagination that was distracting her from her distraction.

Music filled her head from the earbuds on her music player in her pocket. It was set to shuffle, so why did every song that came on go on about sadness, and losing someone, and feeling crazy over loving someone. Something about acting 22 and feeling 17. That's pretty spot on, she told herself. Sasha sadly accepted the realisation that her morning of non-stop housework trying to forget the man of her dreams a complete waste of time. It seemed to her that the only feeling that felt acceptable to her at this point was sadness. She had been telling herself that Col was dangerous, and she was scared, and the safest thing was to leave. So why was the only state of mind she could settle on, total misery

That's it, she told herself, slamming down the glass of water she was holding. She turned the music up, restarted the same song and stormed to her bedroom, frantically searching through the drawer of crap next to her bed for her rabbit, her heart racing and her whole body aching wishing he were there right next to her.. Sasha's hands flowed all over her own torso, with her eyes closed she imagined Col being there, as though he would magically appear next to her, and be lying next to her if she opened her eyes, putting a strong arm under her neck and taking over from her, touching her in all the right places with just the right deftness of touch; holding off from the most important part just until the right moment. It was as though her sleeping dreams had broken through into being daydreams that she couldn't control.

Sasha's hand felt out to her side for the vibrator she'd

thrown onto the bed before collapsing on there herself. The sun was strong today, and streamed through her net curtains onto her bed, warming her up to the extent she could almost feel the heat of his body so close to her.

She thanked God for Aimee's Ann Summer's party just before Christmas. She hadn't intended to buy anything; but the conversation had opened up amongst the increasingly drunken airport girls that by the end any inhibitions from the shyest of girls had been washed away; with tales of Oooh what they'd like to do to Robbie Williams; or how Mel Gibson in his day could have gotten Mina to do just about anything….had he ever wanted to.

Sasha had initially been shocked – nice girls weren't supposed to do these things…..were they? Talking about masturbation and g-spots (She had been most interested to find out about the possible location of the male g-spot – and wondered if she would ever feel confident to bring that up in order to impress the man of her dreams), from blow jobs all the way through to anal and all the toys in between…..

The female songstress's voice crooned slowly and softly, and the gentle guitar strumming lazily along in the background she imagined playing along on a stereo in the corner of the room while imaginary Col's lovemaking played along almost in rhythm with the music.

Sasha's orgasm came almost as soon as she touched her wet vulva with the vibrating phallic synthetic. It was amazing the things she considered doing to and for this man; after having her eyes opened and things suggested to her at that Ann Summer's party (and since – conversations in the office could sometimes turn as blue as their uniforms)

The song ended and her music collection continued to shuffle through random pop songs. Sasha lay crying for the rest of the afternoon. The euphoria of the way the mere thought of him made her body feel gave way to the miserable realisation that she had decided to run away. Once again, she had messed it up.

Where before she had done stupid things like said "I love you" after a one-nighter; or made a fool of herself in front of someone who wasn't interested at a drunken airport party; here was someone who had drawn her in to him, held her closer and more carefully than anyone she had felt before; and someone she had been dreaming about before she had even met him – He was Mr Right; and she had burned her bridges.

Monday morning came as expected. Trains didn't begin in time for an early shift so it was either a car share or a taxi. Sasha hadn't been around the previous week to arrange shares for this week so taxi it was. She'd stopped sobbing enough from the night before to remember to pre-book one. He was sitting outside on the dot at 3.30am. No horns to wake up the neighbours, though, that was the deal. She rode in silence. Nigel, the regular driver from Aerocars, was used to her being quiet before early morning starts. He didn't mind, made a change from the drunken revellers he had been driving home a couple of hours earlier.

"Soooo, good holiday? " Leigh asked, in between applying her lipstick in front of the wall-mounted mirror, as Sasha hanging up her coat in the cloak room.

"Mmmm Yep. " Sasha chipped curtly.

"Didn't hear from you all week – was wondering if everything was OK" Leigh eyed her suspiciously. Sasha looked at her and noticed her knowing expression, blushed slightly and turned away. "Weeeehee I knew it! Holiday romance!!! Tell all!!"

"I can't."

"Oooh…married?"

"No. At least…. No, I don't think so. Just something I fucked up again."

"Oh Sash! No! What happened?"

"Later? "

"Now!" Leigh looked out through the office doors "There's no-one queuing yet…" referring to the passengers for the check-in they were about to open.

"I don't know," Sasha began, "I just…he seems….seemed almost perfect. I think I was just looking for a problem, made one up and scared myself, and left."

"Left?"

"I changed my train ticket and came home a day early"

"Has he called?"

"He doesn't have my number. Or know where I live. I doubt he'd want to find me even if he knew how"

"How thick is that?!"

Mina, their supervisor, clicked her heels along the platform walkway outside the office and entered with her permanent air of authority.

"Why isn't the Corfu Check-In open?" She demanded

"Well, there was no-one waiting so Sasha was just…" Leigh began

"It should have been open 15 minutes ago. Go and set up please." And she disappeared into her back office. A few minutes later, they were loading baggage tags and boarding cards into the printers attached to the check-in computers.

"Apparently there's some kind of meeting called in the top floor conference room this afternoon. There's some bigwigs from Stansted here in Simon's office." Leigh explained.

"Really? For everyone?"

"Yep. All sorts of rumours flying. Downsizing, outsourcing, all sorts" Leigh replied solemnly.

Sasha felt her heart sink. Back at work and trying to

forget about her previous weeks tumultuous break she had almost forgotten how their whole industry was still in shock and damage-control mode.

Leigh had been meaning to call or text her, she told her, to say about the looming visit from Head Office to their branch of Air2Ground handling; but didn't want to interrupt her holiday since she never normally took them.

It was no secret that the whole airline industry had hit hard times since 9/11 and their little team at a small regional airport had noticed some big changes in the past few months.

The stalwarts like Leigh and Sasha and others in the office had been expecting an inevitable downturn in their workload, and that none of their summer holiday season temps would be kept on after the end of September.

It had even got to the point where the Saturday afternoon Jersey got pulled, the last scheduled flight from their airport of what had once been their major customer based there.

Later that day, the entire workforce, landside and airside, had been gathered in the conference room.

"It has come to the point where the decision has been made to close this base." mumbled the short man in the dark suit.

He wasn't much of a presence, a desk-man unused to addressing large crowds, sent down by head office to do their dirty work.

He had been explaining how the company had to scale back their operations after losing numerous contracts for handling, countrywide; as airlines went out of business or else cut routes to save their own overheads.

Their biggest cost-saving measure was to be closing a number of their smaller operations.

This was one.

The gathered colleagues were caught off guard, but the family-like atmosphere in this particular had caught the management off guard also. The assembly of suits made a quick exit after their bombshell, leaving Sasha and her work-mates in a stunned silence.

An hour later, those whose shifts had finished had gathered in Landing Lights. After Pilar had broken down in tears at the bar ordering her drink, and Frenchy learned of their collective job losses, he announced that all of their drinks were free.

They all sat subdued, still in uniform. Against the rules to appear in a drinking establishment in uniform; no-one gave a damn about the rules now.

The group's afternoon drink turned into an afternoon session. Before long, Reuben, their fellow check-in agent and wanabee cabin crew had called Mike, his life-partner and one of the tug drivers from the apron, who was still sober and had gone home to change, had gone round with the spare key to Leigh's place as they were neighbours and close enough to be holders of each other's spare keys, grabbed some of her clothes for her, and spares to lend Sasha.

Some of the others popped home to change, others still (especially the men whose shirts were plain white anyway) had simply removed tell-tale uniform identifications like blazers, ties, bows and so on to appear almost normal, and the commiseration drinks turned into an afternoon session, which went on through into the evening, when they decided to move on from Landing Lights down to the town, where a former colleague had opened a sports-bar-come-nightclub, and always welcomed his old workmates with open arms.

Tonight was karaoke night too; and since that always normal night out, they spent the night singing, crying and shouting into the microphone.

More to Leigh's satisfaction, Sasha had started to open up and talk about this amazing man she had met. They had all found it wonderfully amusing she had fallen for an old Cornish fisherman.

Despite her protests, they all had the set image in their heads of a hunched old man with a long white beard, weathered face, thick cable-knit jumper and sailor's cap, with a pipe sticking out of his mouth.

It certainly hadn't helped that she had only photos of Ol'George and the others, and the boat, on her camera…since Col had been like a ghost any time she was taking photos.

And, the one picture he did appear in, he was bent over hauling a net onto the boat, and the photo was taken from behind; although Leigh gave her a little credit – he had taken his jumper off – those definitely weren't the arms of an old, weathered man.

Leigh began to understand a little of the attraction. It took her another week of persuading to get Sasha to admit she needed to go back. Even just to see him and explain. Leigh had decided that Sasha had just been fishing for discrepancies, to find something wrong, when she had complained over the clandestine 'meeting', the phone call and Col's aversion to being questioned.

Sasha had been the first to admit, when she overheard the phone call, she had been full of enough Scrumpy Jack to allow herself to be willingly fucked to heaven and back in a public place…not that she would have needed much persuasion with her attraction to him; but despite her worries about his dark side…

"Oh shit…" Sasha exclaimed suddenly during their conversation.

"What?" enquired Leigh.

"It was unprotected."

"You were on the edge of a cliff" Leigh giggled.

"I mean….unprotected…" Sasha clarified.

"Oh." Leigh cottoned on "So…..I mean he obviously doesn't sound the type to be sleeping around…."

"OK not so much worried about STDs just yet, although I'll take that up with him if I go..."

"When..." Leigh corrected in between another gulp of the fluorescent green cocktail she was drinking.

"When. But...well...you know..."

"Oh Sash....you don't think..."

"Um, not due until this week sometime. God Leigh I can't go back to find him, make up and dump a pregnancy on him! He'd definitely run a mile!" Sasha picked up the three-quarters-full pint that was in front of her, about to drink. Leigh looked at her and slowly raised an eyebrow, as though to ask 'should you really be drinking?'.

Sasha pursed her lips and put the drink down, dejected. There went her night. She went to the bar and ordered a cup of tea, and was met with some very odd looks. She just shook her head to confirm she wasn't going to explain herself.

Somehow, Sasha didn't feel like she minded not getting completely sozzled like the rest of them. It was as though her predicament was enough to drown out the miserable news they'd had in work. She was happy to let everyone else carry on drinking to drown theirs – maybe it was a good thing – it seemed alcohol had gotten her into this situation in the first place.

The next morning, Leigh went to the pharmacy for Sasha; and that afternoon they both heaved a sigh of relief at the negative home pregnancy test. They had two days off now, so celebrated that evening with pizza and a bottle of wine to make up for Sasha's enforced sobriety the night before. The one bottle turned in to three, and watching rom-com chick-flicks on some random movie channel they found as they flicked through Leigh's cable channels. By 10pm they were both in floods of tears over lost loves and rom-com heroes and, well, just from the wine, really. In her one moment of lucidity during the evening, Sasha looked in the bathroom mirror, after bringing up half a pizza with the aid of some of the cheap wine, and felt grateful for having a good friend to see this through with.

Three days later Sasha's period began – the most welcome one she had ever had. There was a fleeting moment of sadness…a vision of having children with Col and being happy and content. Then realising her current situation would definitely not have been the way to begin that particular journey.

11

On the first Monday morning in May, Sasha stood at the bar and smiled at Martha who seemed happier to see her than would normally have been expected.

"Any chance of a room, Martha?"

"Back then?" Martha grinned at her.

"For a few days. I realised I have a bit of unfinished business…"

At that moment, Martha looked past her and smiled and nodded to a stranger who had entered the bar, and before Sasha noticed, he was staring at her dangerously.

Upon closer inspection; Sasha was knocked off her feet to recognise the strong frame of Col Tangye, clean shaven, without the thick beard that had adorned his face since they had met.

He looked even better than she remembered. Sasha's heart skipped a beat. Or ten.

Colan's expression should have been a warning for her to stay away. He stared daggers at her and then turned on his heels and left. Martha watched and shook her head.

The older woman looked at Sasha and cocked her head in the direction of the door.

"I'll put yer bag in yer room for ye. Go."

The sunny days that had greeted Sasha during her previous week here had passed. This British summer was looking to be the regular tumultuous cloudy, miserable season that sent so many people rushing to her airport boarding flights to Spain and Greece and anywhere else that saw the forgotten sun more often than the UK.

The clouds rolled in the sky so much so that Col's anger seemed to be controlling the weather, So I'm comparing him to a God now? Sasha chastised herself as she walked with her head bowed a little against the wind, before realising she had come to a halt for an obstacle, and what she was actually staring at was his heaving, prominent chest a little closer than she should have been; considering her eyes were filling with water at the sudden shock of being thrust into his line of sight.

Col had never expected this. He had been angry she had left but quickly saw, after a few days at sea and swallowing back into his own private world, that she had, in fact, saved herself.

She didn't need to get embroiled in what he was doing – he wasn't so much worried about what trouble he would get in to, but she could get into danger. And danger for her would hurt him just as much.

Not to mention breaking everything he'd been working

towards for the past 3 years. Unbeknownst to them, a few concerned faces had gathered to watch through the inn's small, time-frosted windows, Martha at the front.

Fuck this, Col gave in, marched forward and kissed Sasha hard as the heavens opened on them. The fierce and longing-filled kiss seemed to last forever – at least long enough for Martha to beam ecstatically and shoo everyone away from the windows, to leave the young 'uns to their…well, whatever they got up to next…

When they parted, and finally noticed the rain, Col dragged Sasha by her hand to his truck across the road and they dived in, more to shelter from the rain, than to actually drive anywhere.

"Sorry" he muttered, not looking at her, staring straight ahead through the waterlogged window as streaks of rain soaked it.

"Sorry. I'm sorry. I should never have run away like that."

"I don't even have your number" Col seemed for a moment like a child whose parent had left him behind somewhere; more hurt by her than angry at her.

"I…I don't know what scared me but I couldn't think. I think I may have taken that phone call a little the wrong way…"

"Phone call?"

"At Newlyn…..behind the toilets….I had had too much

to drink, my friend Leigh said it was probably nothing and even if it sounded bad there…"

"Sasha, forget about the phone call."

"OK, but it was just the whole thing with that meeting you had arranged too, it just seemed odd." Col almost cut in to correct her but she continued, hardly taking a breath, from fear and nerves, and trying to vent her frustrations. "But then Leigh reminded me how little I know about your life or the lifestyle down here and told me off…I mean I jumped to conclusions…I jumped to conclusions about you when I first saw you and look at you now…..you're no ancient mariner…and…." She stopped and took a breath and looked at him again. "…and fuck, you look good without a beard". She stopped, and breathed deeply.

Now it was Col's turn to stare, longingly, at her heaving chest, the v-neck t-shirt she was wearing was almost soaked through and her breasts almost clearly visible through it, her wet hair hanging loosely, and one shoulder of her shirt hanging off casually.

"OK that wasn't quite as bad as I thought it was going to be." She sighed.

Col, strong silent Col, smiled at her with a twinkle in his eye.

"It's been bugging me for a while." He muttered.

"What?" Sasha queried.

"The beard" he grinned. Sasha laughed, more at the relief that the mood had been lightened.

"What on earth possessed you to grow a beard anyway? I mean…"She looked at him, slyly and flirtatiously, "…a bit of designer stubble….ooh yes, that would look nice. But THAT thing? "

"Designer stubble, eh? " Col checked himself in the rear view mirror "You think?"

"Hot." Sasha approved. "Don't get me wrong, the other one tickled… but…."

Col raised an eyebrow at her comically. Sasha smiled. They sat in an almost comfortable silence for a few moments. The rain hammered on the car. Sasha frowned as a thought occurred, "I don't even know where you live!"

"Ah, well, that's the thing…" Col replied, seriousness returning to his tone. "At the moment I don't actually live anywhere…"

"Huh?" Sasha was a little confused. "I was renting a room from Ol' George but his nephew has come in to town and I gave it up fer 'im."

"So, where are you staying now?"

"Well…." He paused, and looked up at the Inn, The Sailors Rest. Sasha felt her heart skip a beat.

"You're staying here?" have all my birthdays come at once?

“Kind of. I have some work to do overnight though so…” Col sighed, glanced back at her wet t-shirt “I won’t be around tonight…” Sasha followed his gaze and suddenly realised about her wet shirt. She pulled it forward and shook it off a little in a vain attempt to dry it slightly.

“But I’ll pick you up at 7 tomorrow? The Lifeboat crew are having a fundraiser over at Sennen Village hall.”

Sasha grinned, and looked at him. Col decided she hadn’t looked so sweet until that moment – genuinely happy and relaxed.

“I’ll be waiting” She half leaned towards him, and he her.

For some reason, they were both faltering, slightly, an awkward moment where two people who had been as intimate as they had suddenly weren’t sure if they were an item or not or what they were….

“OK.” He acknowledged. After a few more moments of discomfort, Col took the lead.

“Right. I’m gonna kiss you now ok?”

“Please do” she all but jumped across the cab onto his lap.

They delved into each other’s mouths, euphoria setting in at the taste and feel of being this close again, without the tenseness of the previous hungry attack in the rain. Sasha had to come up for air after a couple of minutes but Col dragged her back to him. Col wished he could stay here with her and let her go just to see what they could possibly get up to in this cab – he was pretty sure Sasha had an ability to get up to a number of things he had dreamed of her; plus a few he had never even imagined possible.

But he woke up from his trance and realised time must be getting away from him, looking at his watch behind her head while trying not to make her stop kissing him, he finally had to put an end to it.

“Sasha…mmmm…..oh, shit….Sash…I can’t…”

“You have to go?” she sat back a little and smiled a sad but understanding smile at him, batting her eyelids.

“When you put it like that I wish I didn’t.” He stroked his solid hands down her back, making her spine tingle.

“I do have to come in to pick up stuff from my room though,” She grinned mischievously in response.

They hurriedly got out of the cab and ran through the rain into the Inn. The hotchpotch of a gathering inside seemed to have suddenly turned to looking busy with something else the moment the door opened. Martha suddenly backed away from the window with the best view of the van and collected glasses like she’d been doing it for hours. Two farmers in the corner bowed their heads in deep conversation and tried to look like they had been ignoring everyone for hours.

Sasha smiled knowingly at Martha.

"I'll get your key, love" Martha told her. "You're in the same room again."

"I'll be away again tonight, Martha," Col offered, quite pointedly, to ensure she knew nothing remotely interesting was likely to be happening under her roof tonight, at least.

"Aw OK love. Breakfast?"

"No ta…I'll not be back till 'late."

Martha looked quite put out after her hope of the past hour or so.

"Alright Col, thanks for letting me know." She turned to Sasha "Doesn't like me to worry if he doesn't come back. Least if I know it's planned we got some kind of understanding." Suddenly a thought dawned on her "You'll be here tonight though?"

Sasha grinned understanding her suggestion "of course!"

Col had gone ahead through the door to the rickety staircase that went up the back of the building. Sasha hung back while Martha scurried to get her a room key from behind the bar.

"Your bag's already up there. " She said "had one of the lads lug it up fer me earlier" Sasha smiled sweetly at the landlady and scurried through the door.

To her surprise someone grabbed her arm from behind a door and pushed her towards the staircase. She turned slightly to realise it was Col with a gleam in his eye. He pushed her up the staircase, slapping her behind playfully. She giggled and reached her door, fumbling with the key as he nibbled the back of her neck.

He followed her in and kissed her again, this time arms roaming up and down the back of her body. He looked around the room as much as he could without detaching from her face.

“Mmmmmm… nice room” he mumbled into her mouth.

“Nice view of those hunky fishermen down in the cove when the boats come in of a morning” She replied. Col leaned back away from her and smiled. Sasha winked at him.

“Thought you were in a hurry” Sasha probed. He glanced at his watch,

“Oh yep” schoolboy childishness putting a spring back in his step “here…” he bent over a small notepad and pencil on the small table in the corner and scribbled his number down.

“Will ye PLEASE text me your number so I don’t lose you again?” He pleaded. She nodded wholeheartedly. Sasha picked up her phone as he left and started tapping in his number.

He rushed next door; she could hear him clattering around the room getting whatever it was he was after. Sasha moved out to the corridor just as he came back out, locking his door behind him and slinging on a heavy looking long waxed coat over his shoulders, under a wide brimmed hat. She inhaled deeply to calm her nerves, as he strode across the landing in one step, looking like some hero from one of Leigh's breaktime novels.

Half expecting him to kiss her again, he seemed to take pleasure in leaving her something as basic as a wink and a cheeky grin as he passed her, playfully. But it made her heart leap to see him prance down the stairs with a skip in his step, the man she thought sometimes held dark secrets and kept so much bottled up inside. His being happy appealed to her to keep him that way. Sasha sighed, went back into her room and threw herself back on the bed; now so incredibly happy she had come back at Leigh's insistence; using up more of her leave, since she'd only lose it or be forced to take it before they were closed down for good, in November.

The bittersweet pang hit her and the rain that was thundering against her window as she looked out across the cove – her life as she knew it at home was about to change.

She should be out there looking for a new job; but instead she had come here – although Leigh's logic was hey, if something is going to happen, don't you want to be where Col is?

Sasha began wondering if maybe there was a future down here with him. She had heard about the Cornish economy not being great but surely there was something she could do, plus his roots weren't so solid here that they couldn't move together and start a new life somewhere together.

Oh great, I'm doing it again she thought, planning on ahead a whole life with someone I barely know. For all I know he's in it for the sex, like the others, and once anything else gets in the way he'll be packing me off home telling me his life is no place for a woman again…. Sasha chastised herself, told herself to stop.

Nothing was anything until she knew – she had come down here to talk to him; if she could keep herself from touching him they might get something discussed, to see if Leigh was right. In the meantime, her return had been almost amazing although she thanked God she had brought the Rabbit with her even if just for this first day.

Tomorrow he'd be back; and in the very next room… As she stared out the window a huge flash of lightening cracked the sky in half and startled her. A huge clap of thunder rolled in behind it. She could see his truck roll up the hill, and out of the village. She had a strange, sinking feeling. I hope nothing happens to him… She hated not knowing where he was going.

12

Col lay on his stomach, overlooking a secluded cove, with a pair of binoculars, hidden between a couple of rocks offering him a little protection from the weather, along with most lines of sight. He'd been here all night, partly under a tarp cover when it had been dark and the bright blue wouldn't stand out against the night. He was sure this was the location he had garnered from Juan. He'd been watching for over 24 hours and nothing, no proof at all.

He was glad there was no movement in the location he had been sent to observe. Had there been, his state of distraction would have led him to possibly mess this up completely.

All he could feel was the tightness in his groin, pushing against his trousers, made all the more uncomfortable by having to stay close to the ground.

Every time he thought of her - although all the more concentrated having just seen her and felt her and touched her – he got like this. He was getting increasingly more scared that he'd throw the towel in completely, tell his superiors to stuff it and run away with her. After all this time, all the preparation…

He suddenly noticed movement down on the beach, around the point where the rocks got a little rougher… He grabbed his binoculars. Just a couple of fool-hardy touring adventure fishermen, clambering around the head trying to get the best catch. There were too many of these men were getting themselves into fixes after watching extreme fishing shows abundant on some of the cable channels these days. He had heard tales over beers from friends in the coastguard.

Col shrugged, this wasn't what he was here for. His mobile vibrated in his pocket. He groaned at the sensation, so close to his throbbing erection. This wasn't helping.

He grinned when he saw the message. Thinking it would be from the boss, it was from Sasha – kind of poetic justice then, the response he'd had to the vibration.

'Can't wait till later xxx this is my number… S'

He clicked the option to save contact and saved her number under a simple 'S' and deleted the message. He scrolled through the contacts list and found "HQ" and sent them a message.

'No movement at expected rendezvous. Dep +9 days. Crossing and handover taking longer?'

Once again, once sent, he went to his 'sent items' folder and deleted that message too.

At the same time, in Liverpool docks, customs officers were busy inspecting inbound container vessels. Martin King watched them intently from an elevated position on one of the ships.

“Nothing untoward today then, Martin?” Craig Hooper, the captain of MV Neopol asked him.

“Not yet, Captain.” Martin waved at one of his men down on the dock side. The man shook his head ‘no’ and shrugged. Martin nodded. He checked his phone, and saw Col’s message:

‘No movement at expected rendezvous. Dep +9 days. Crossing and handover taking longer?’

Martin hated being told the obvious by his team. He nodded to the captain and disembarked. He replied to Col’s message.

‘Stand down. Return normal ops’

On top of the cliff in Cornwall, Col’s phone vibrated again.

Excitement rushed through his veins expecting it to be more words from Sasha. Dejectedly he read Martin’s message and deleted it.

He checked his watch. About bloody time. Col deleted the message from his phone and practically ran to his truck. He made a quick change into some fresh clothes he'd slung into the back, knowing he didn't want to waste a minute more away from Sasha.

13

Col arrived back outside the 'Rest' at exactly the moment Sasha had appeared in the bar, wearing a mid-length summer dress, although a little too see-through and cold to wear it on its own, she had a petticoat slip underneath it. Jimmy had noticed straight away – Martha noticed him noticing and gave him a warning look.

"You look very lovely, Sasha!" She said, beaming. Sasha felt a little flushed at the attention. She brightened up as Col barged through the door.

Col was a little taken aback by the vision he encountered. It wasn't as though she needed to dress to impress him; he was pretty much decided about Sasha and the way she made him feel. But she had put on a little mascara, wore a loosely fitting flowing dress that allowed her best features to stand out; and had left her hair loose, hanging down over her shoulder on one side, instead of the loose knot she normally held it up in. Sasha's eyes sparkled when she noticed Col. She smiled at him, then blushed sweetly at his expression and looked down.

Col found it strangely endearing – feeling a little queasy at his sappy behaviour. How could someone who turned him on so much physically, be penetrating his soul and making him feel things that sappy heroes in romantic novels and 'chick flicks' were always described as experiencing, to make the girls go weak at the knees. He felt like a pubescent school boy again. He became uncomfortably aware of the physical connotations that entailed – knowing he'd have to leave the public place pretty soon or else his body would betray him.

He sauntered forward as confidently as he could, hands in his pockets; mostly to hold the crotch of his jeans forward as much as he could; partly to try and seem as nonchalant and relaxed as possible.

He wasn't fooling anyone. Even Derek and Steve in the corner were amused by the younger man's efforts.

"Ready?" He enquired of Sasha, leaning one of his arms towards her without removing the hand from his pocket; offering it to her to sling her own arm through. Sasha beamed a confident smile at him again and slung her hand daintily through. "See you later Martha, Jimmy," she called as they sauntered towards the door, waving her free hand.

Col turned on the radio as he started the engine, Sasha sat back, happy, relaxed, excited and recognised the song on the radio, "There's nothing like this…." sang the soulful voice from the early nineties. Sasha bobbed her head, dancing along, and singing along with the chorus. Col smiled amusedly at her, and drove away, up out of the village towards Sennen. The party was already in full swing when they got there. Col paid for two entries at the door as Sasha wandered in ahead. She was amazed by what she saw. Expecting a small gathering of old locals, stuck in their ways and disorganised, in a barn filled with hay, she found a buzzing, vibrant hall, decorated in the colours of the Royal National Lifeboat Institution , ribbons and bows and balloons and a huge disco-ball having been rigged up over the dance floor. The DJ on the stage was playing lively, up-beat but recognisable music like the best type of wedding DJ who could keep everyone happy from Great-Granny to the youngest of pageboys.

He had "Buster's Karaoke and Party" emblazoned across the front of his equipment on the stage at the end of the hall. A makeshift bar had been set up to the side of the room, but a good one at that – small beer fridges were being kept stocked up by the busy women behind the table-clothed trestles, they seemed to have all sorts of food and drink available and no shortage of people ordering. Sasha wandered along to the wall next to the refreshments. Another table had been set up with information on the donations they had collected in order to be auctioned off in a silent auction later on. The Sennen Lifeboat, "R.N.L.B. City of London III " was manned by local crew, and well supported – Colan described to her how fundraising helped keep the Lifeboat operational for when it was needed, and since everyone knew everyone else around here, everyone clubbed together to help with the fundraising.

Sasha began to see another side to Col. He schmoozed with the best of them, everyone loved him. Not an ounce of the surly, gruff sailor he was during his work on the trawler.

She stood in the corner on her way back from the toilet at one point and just watched him. He acted so genuine with everyone. He blended in.

To her when they were alone together, he was gorgeous, strong, tall, dark and ruggedly handsome with the piercing eyes that melted her into submission; but he also looked perfectly at home around here, among other seamen and farmers and proper Cornish country people. Salt of the earth. What more could she ask for – perfect man in every way – in bed (or wherever), in public. Leigh had been a good friend to send her back here, with the advice of thinking about her future. Sasha decided she should maybe broach the subject of life path.

Col took her around the room, seemingly showing her off to all and sundry. She sparkled with enthusiasm and for some reason she felt they were the centre of attention for the evening. After the initial introductions, Sasha hardly noticed time passing. Between chatting to people and dancing; and joining in the banter between everyone as to whether anyone was brave enough to get up and do some Karaoke; she felt coveted by Col, who seemed to be watching her closely every time she glanced in his direction.

He would rest a protective hand on her behind whenever he was near. She was sat on a table with two of the lifeboat wives when Col brought her a drink over and sat down next to them. The two women, Sandy and Janet, seemed as though they would have loved to stay and chat with Col a bit more; but they got called up by the Karaoke DJ – “Time for a bit o’Dolly Parton, Ladies?” he called as the intro to “9to5”struck up.

Sasha felt a little relieved to be finally sat alone with Col. She looked at him watching the women giggle while trying to sing up on the stage and laughed at their attempts jovially. Sasha mulled over in her mind the best way to strike up this conversation. Hey, the sex is great, ever thought about moving in together?

Nope. God this wasn’t the best idea, was it?

Great, I’m considering scaring a guy off by telling him I’m dropping everything to be near him…? Hey, I’m about to lose my job, thinking about moving here permanently and…..

“So, how was home when you got back? “ Col broke into her thoughts. “Oh.” Sasha was startled

“Sorry, deep in thought, were ya?” he smiled.

“We lost our jobs” Sasha said, sadly.

Col wasn’t quite sure how to respond to that. Taken aback slightly, he paused for a moment. Torn between the excitement of knowing she had nothing really to go back for and was free to do what she wanted and wanting to tell her to stay with him forever, after all, I'm not going to be here forever, he told himself; or keeping quiet, letting her go back to her own life and making her own decisions.

"That was one of the reasons I came back, really,"

"Why, 'coz you didn't have to work?"

"Oh no we don't close down 'till December. I'm using up more leave. Leigh, my best mate at work, persuaded me to come back…" Sasha paused, for courage mainly, and looked at him "to see where we lay."

Col raised an eyebrow, amused

"Not sure that sounds right?" "Um…" She blushed "I mean, We…um…I've really enjoyed…" Sasha frowned, trying to phrase it correctly, and still sound like a 'good' girl. "What we have is amazing; at least, I think so. I just wondered, if for some reason I were to move, well, let's say, consider moving away from home…"

Col sat in silence, much to her dismay his face unreadable, his green eyes piercing into her. Just as she was about to begin, the DJ piped up as the previous pop song died down, "Where's Sasha? Is Sasha here?" She looked up, surprised. Sandy waved frantically at her and nodded.

"Over there? The girls have nominated you up next"

Sasha's eyes widened in shock – she didn't know anyone here. She'd only drunk half of one glass of cider

– this was hardly an airport night out at The Sports Bar Karaoke night where they all got up and had a go, after having already drunk all night.

"Come on love, you said you'd done a bit – give us a tune!"Janet shouted over at her.

Col looked at her challengingly, very interested to hear this.

"Really?" he asked, sitting back, crossing his arms and motioning for her to take the floor.

Sasha took that as a dare from him and stood up defiantly, unable to help the smile that spread across her face when a large proportion of the hall cheered for her in support.

"Right then, I'll put on another tune while you decide then you're up next" boomed the DJ into the microphone. Sasha went up to him and started browsing through the folders he'd put together.

He seemed about to give her some suggestions but she noticed one that caught her attention. "You think that one's too slow for the party?" She pointed out to him. "Nah, easy going bunch they'll hum along I suppose." "OK then" she smiled.

Col was deep in discussions with two of the lifeboat crew about a picture of the current boat that had been enlarged and hung on the wall, when the strains of a popular love song from the late nineties piped up and the babble died down throughout the hall as Sasha started singing.

A little nervous, she began a little quiet, but gradually seemed to forget her surroundings, and glanced less and less at the audience watching her intently; and less and less at the words flashing up on the screen before her. She knew this song and knew the words – it was her go-to end of the night song when out with the gang - she she'd only been reading them off the screen for comfort.

It helped about half way through that someone lowered the main hall light and the disco lights shone that little but brighter; reflecting off the disco ball on the ceiling, giving her something else to look at and concentrate on, forgetting her surroundings and singing, every now and again, searching the room for Col, it seemed to her there was no-one else in the room and she was singing directly to him.

It helped further that various couples had started slow dancing along to the song, so she didn't feel like everyone was gawking at her.

Col watched with interest to start with; the further she got into the song the more her voice mesmerised him, and for the first time ever he concentrated on the words and understood what she was singing.

Maybe it was crazy, they both felt like teenagers, even though, she was almost 30. God, he himself was almost 40. For some reason that did it for him. He'd never been much of a romantic and hadn't really listened to much "girly" music before, but something about the gleam in

Sasha's eyes as she finished to an enthusiastic cheer and blushed, her flushed expression, made him need her there and then.

She floated down the stairs at the side of the stage, Col excused himself from those he'd been chatting with, held her firmly by the arm and led her towards the exit. Sasha read the expression on his face and entirely went with it. The purpose in his movement and urgency in his step was making getting Sasha excited just from the brisk walk to the car park. He pulled her around and slammed her up against the cab of the truck.

The strength of his chest pinning her to the car and the determined look in his eyes nearly pushed her to the brink there and then. She could feel his arousal growing against her through the material of her dress and his jeans. He stared playfully down into her eyes,

"I need you now" he whispered.

"I gathered," She answered "But…here?"

"Good point," he said, looking around.

"Get in," he ordered her, and climbed into the cab, slamming the door, starting the engine feverishly. They drove and drove for what seemed like forever as Sasha shifted in her seat in vain attempts to stop her juices making too much of a mess of her clothes and the seat. The more she tried to calm herself down, the more excited she got. The mere thought that the promise of him could do this to her was enough to bring her to the brink of an orgasm.

Col finally stopped the car and got out. Almost leaping over the bonnet he opened her door and took her seductively by the hand and helped her out. He kissed her softly and sweetly before leading her to the back of the truck. What on earth is he doing? She wondered. He began to pull off the tarp cover that was hooked over the back. Col winked at her, and lifted her into the back of the pickup, almost without effort. She knelt there as he jumped in himself, and looking around her, she realised the back of the pickup had been made up like a bed, complete with mattress, quilt and pillows. And surprisingly clean at that. She stared at him.

"Who has a bed in the back of a pickup truck?!"She exclaimed "Someone who knows he'll need it at short notice" he murmured as he crawled towards her and began kissing her passionately whilst forcing her to move backwards and lie down.

Col somehow magically managed to relieve her of her dress without letting go of her lips, or to be more precise, her neck, and cleavage, and naval, and…

Oh my goodness, Sasha's eyes rolled at the sensation as Col, still fully clothed, had reached her thighs and kissed them repetitively while he removed her knickers. He looked back at her with a playfully wicked grin on his face and winked at her. Sasha threw her head back in anticipation and he straddled her, pinning her chest down with his thighs. He began tantalisingly slowly, circling the tip of his tongue around her clitoris. Sasha felt the urge to reach out and touch him. She ran her hands along his calf muscles. Even through his jeans they were impressive. This man must be a God of some kind!

She moved her hands along his thighs and up onto the muscular mounds of his buttocks. She cupped them in her hands and squeezed, as much as she could – again they seemed to be composed of pure muscle. Col replaced his tongue with a finger on her clitoris and moved his mouth back, and plunged his tongue deep inside her.

Sasha writhed with pleasure, trying to curb her gasps from becoming too loud, which only turned him on all the more. He moved his own hands around and placed them on her exposed buttocks and discovered he could control his mastery of her vagina all the more from that position. Sasha found she had to stop concentrating on his rear end and throw her arms out to the sides and grab the mattress with all her might, biting her lips to stop from screaming in ecstasy in goodness knows whatever public place they were in.

Col felt he was on a mission to make this woman love him unconditionally now. Before she moved or stayed anywhere she'd have to find out about him and he knew she wasn't going to like it. He had to prove to her he was worth looking past it. Judging by the wetness between her legs, and the gyrating movements her pelvis was making, he was doing something right. He slowly inserted one finger after another to join his tongue, while still massaging her clitoris with his other hand.

Before long he heard Sasha fail to hold her tongue as she

had been doing and cried out as her body convulsed. Col expertly leapt off her and turned around so he was lying next to her, lifted her shoulders so he was holding her in his arms and kissed her hotly. Sasha hungrily kissed him back, licking and sucking his lips and his tongue and running her tongue over his teeth, exploring his mouth that she was getting so used to and erotically tasting her own juices from his mouth.

"Wow" Sasha gasped as she lay back for a little breather.

"You OK?" he whispered

"Amazing" she whispered back "Col, where did you learn that?!"

It didn't seem like she was expecting an answer. He grinned and winked at her. They lay side by side in silence for a while, staring at the stars. Thankful it had stopped raining earlier in the day and didn't seem to be threatening to begin again anytime soon.

Sasha recovered herself enough to decide to repay the favour.

Without a word, she knelt up over Col and began to undo his jeans. He looked down and watched with interest, raising his midriff up a little so she could take his trousers down. Col put his hands behind his head and rested it on his biceps, with his head raised he watched her with ardent interest. Sasha slowed down, teasing him shockingly, enough for him to close his eyes and gasp a little.

She slipped her fingers under the waistband of his boxer, but instead of instantly pulling them down, she spent time sliding her fingers around the width of the waistband that she had access to. She slowly peeled them down his thighs and legs and over his feet. She shot him a seductive, determined look then bent her head over his crotch. Here goes nothing she told herself, remember everything Marie talked about… One of the conversations she'd been privy to in the office once had centred around one of the girls describing how she had been taught to give blow jobs "See, I didn't realise you were supposed to stick it down your throat…"

Since then, Cosmopolitan had been her friend and she loved internet research; but as yet she'd been a little too shy when encounters arose that she'd never put any of it into practice.

Col was making her confidence soar and she wanted to do things with him, and to him, she had never considered with anyone else before, ever.

Sasha held his erection in her hand and stroked it gently with the tip of her finger, getting up the courage.

Bit late to back out now, she told herself, I've come this far he's expecting it.

She carefully touched the tip of his penis with her tongue, and for some reason delighted when it twitched slightly. OK, I must have done something right.

Her confidence boosted and a naughty grin sweeping over her face, she chewed her bottom lip a little, and then licked further down the side of his member, twirled her tongue a little around the base and up the other side. Col let out a small grunt and placed a hand on the back of her head, stroking her hair.

Sasha began to enjoy herself and the effect she seemed to be having on him – he certainly wasn't fighting her off. She wasn't really sure of what to do next, she knew she'd read a few tips but she was in no state to remember details at the moment.

She decided to go for it. After flicking her tongue once or twice around the tip, she slowly and carefully closed her lips around the end of his penis. She knew he was well endowed from their previous encounters, but it hadn't occurred to her to wonder at this point how she was supposed to get the whole thing in her mouth. Maybe that wasn't the point.

She moved her tongue around the organ while she began to move her head up and down in a slow rhythm, after a few goes she changed the rhythm and sped a little. Col's hand grabbed her hair and tugged a little, letting her know she was still doing well; or at least down the right lines.

Sasha came up for air for a moment and gazed at him seductively again, then ducked down towards his crotch again. She gathered all of her courage and determination and allowed his erection to fill her mouth completely, then carefully opened her throat to allow the tip to penetrate further. Sasha thanked heaven she'd at least tried this before, even if just practice on a small banana, before graduating to her Rampant Rabbit.

Col felt like his mind was about to explode – he'd never expected this. The sensations she was creating in his guts were indescribable – things he'd definitely never experienced before.

His free hand moved down to grab her hair as well, gripping tightly her soft curls as she worked so seemingly effortlessly. Where on earth had she come from?

Col felt his orgasm building inside him and couldn't hold it any more. Lost in sublime ecstasy, his semen shot into her mouth as she raised her head just in time. She closed her mouth around the head so as not to spill any.

A little unsure, but having read it was only polite to swallow; she did so, obediently, wiped her lips gently with her fingers then sat back on her knees. It took Col a moment to come around from staring blankly, open-mouthed, up to the sky. Eventually, he turned to her expectant face. "Was that OK? "She asked, quietly, bringing her legs out from under her and laying down next to him on her side, facing him.

"OK? " He gasped, turning to look her in the eye "OK? You fucking blew my mind!" He was astounded at what had just happened.

"Good" She said quietly, biting her bottom lip again nervously, "Coz I've never done it before"

Col laughed out loud.

"You're kidding me?!" He couldn't believe it "Where the hell do you learn how to do that?"

Sasha shrugged, "I work with some interesting people." She smiled mischievously at him.

Recognising the mock accusing look he shot her she quickly added, "The girls. They talk a lot in the office, not very censored."

Col raised his torso up again and rolled over to cover her protectively. He began to kiss her again, tantalisingly slowly. She kissed him back, and then, feeling his erection growing against her leg again, stopped to look him in the eye.

"Really? Already?" her eyes glistened with a smile. Col winked at her. Something dawned on Sasha and she stopped suddenly.

"Wait…we need to…"

"What?" he cut in, impatiently, as he breathed into her neck. Sasha sat up and took a breath, then looked at him a little more seriously.

"After I went home, last time, I realized…it struck me we hadn't really been paying attention to…practical stuff"

"Practical stuff?" Col cottoned on. "Ah."

"I feel really bad, bringing it up…"

"No, don't , sensible."

"It's just, after last time, I spent a little while going out of my mind with worry about…unplanned pregnancies…and…stuff." Col was silent for a little while. His mind suddenly started going off on a tangent after her comment about pregnancy - babies…children….a family?

With Sasha?

A little smile crept across his lips. It scared him slightly that he was suddenly mulling the idea over in his head as a possibility; as opposed to immediately pushing it away as being out of the question.

The matter of 'settling down' had come up more and more often any time he was home visiting his mother.

"You are getting older Col, like it or not. You should find a nice girl and settle down…". Col shook his head to get rid of the image of his mother and the sound of her voice.

"Look, just to set your mind at ease, I don't have any…anything you could catch," he assured her.

"Good." She nodded. "Me neither."

"Good." Col looked at her, and admitted, mostly to himself, "But we really don't want to risk…"

"Babies." She finished for him. He nodded. Col looked around, wondering what they could do about the situation. They were parked in the deserted car park outside the Land's End hotel complex, in a dark corner away from the view of the road. It occurred to him there may be a vending machine in the toilets in the hotel. Taking a moment to gather energy to head in the direction of the hotel, he wondered if he should broach the subject of futures.

"Do you ever think about children?" He asked, trying his best to make it sound light-hearted. Sasha was a little taken aback.

"Um…not really. Not yet. I mean, I always assumed I will have children. I haven't really thought about it to be honest. I just assumed I'd meet someone, get married first." Sasha bit her lip to stop herself, chastising herself for her mouth running away with her. Too much information? She thought, is this getting a little awkward now?

"You know how we were talkin' earlier" Col carried on.

"Not sure I can think back that long!" Sasha replied "but, kind of. What about it? I mean, I didn't mean to scare you, or probe. It's just, I think…it might almost be time for me to make big changes in my life and…I just thought, given us…getting along like we have been…whether there was any…future possible."

"You know I've got a bit going on at the moment…" Col said, after a pause.

"I gathered." Sasha tried to sound matter-of-fact, but looked down to avoid catching his eye

"Look, I think I'm … I mean we… obviously have a

mutual attraction and…possible feelings… for each other…" Col stuttered, trying to avoid using scary words he couldn't even bring himself to think of himself, let alone say to her.

Sasha wasn't so strong to suppress it "Yes, and I think I'm in love with you" She blurted out, wincing as soon as she said it.

Col stared at her, expressionlessly. If she had hoped to read something in his eyes, a glimmer of recognition, of reciprocated feelings, she got nothing. In fact, when he grunted, jumped off the truck and stormed off towards the hotel, she pretty much saw this as having completely scared him off.

Great, now I've done it. Except she had no choice but to sit in his truck and wait for him to return, since it was the middle of the night and she had no way of getting back to Tregiffen. It must be almost 2am by now. Staying in the truck was probably safest anyway. Sasha could have kicked herself. Well, she thought, at least it wouldn't be as hard to walk away this time since she's really put her foot in it.

She couldn't have been more wrong in her assumptions of him. Col had been so caught off guard by her admission, it was enough to make him walk away; but so welcoming and accepting of what she had blurted out, it was so much what he wanted to hear that he knew he needed to go and get those condoms from the vending machine right now.

Sasha lay down on the mattress, curled up in the quilt for warmth she hadn't realised she needed until she was left alone and stared up at the stars, planning her trip home.

She contemplated what she should start looking for at the Job Centre on Monday. Go back to the admin section? She was becoming quite a good PA and office manager at a store on an industrial estate outside the city before giving up her full-time, permanent job there to take a chance on a summer temp job.

But the summer temp job had looked so appealing – it was at an Airport! How exciting, glamorous, the endless possibilities of travel and seeing the world and mingling with elite and famous… It hadn't been, glamorous that is.

But despite the long hours, stupid-o-clock start times, Sasha had become addicted to the adrenaline filled buzz of the place, the noise of the aircraft, the camaraderie of the crews and the ground staff. She really was going to miss that place, and had no idea what she wanted now. Her only other obsession (which had begun to top her work place) was Col. That conclusion and thinking his name again brought her back down to earth.

Tears began to well up and she turned over to bury her face in the pillow. Sasha breathed in deeply, remnants of the small of him embedded in the soft material. She snaked her arms around the pillow for comfort and hugged it closer to her. It took her a few moments to realise something was odd. Her hand under the pillow had fallen on a strange shaped object. Cold hard metal greeted her hand instead of the wooden panels that lined the bottom of flat bed.

Sasha had never seen a real gun before. Only toy plastic ones he brother had played with; and a mock up they'd been shown by Security at the airport once during an induction talk. She held it in her hands and stared at it blankly, confused for a moment. After what seemed like an age, it sank in that she was holding a real pistol.

She had no idea what kind but there could be no doubting it was real. Not a hunting weapon, rifle, not anything that a fisherman in Cornwall would need for....anything. She knew that much.

Criminals used these things, muggers, terrorists. Images of the dubious things she had tried to push out of her mind flashed back. Col's angry flashes, secret meetings, disappearing overnight, suspect phone calls ... This had to be enough.

She may have scared him away but he was lying. He had to be. He'd been lying the whole time. Not just to her, but to everyone in the village – he was a newcomer 3 years ago, they didn't know anything about him and just accepted him. Perfectly possible he came in with a hidden agenda.

Sasha jumped down from the truck. Before she knew which direction to go in she saw him in the distance sauntering back towards the truck. The sky was beginning to pale although his face was still in the dark.

His huge imposing frame striding confidently in her

direction created a sinister image. Sasha lost it, turned in the opposite direction and ran. She didn't even notice she was still holding the gun in her hand.

14

Sasha ran and ran until Col's larger strides caught up with her and grabbed her arm. She pulled out the gun and threw it onto the ground in front of him. Col jumped angrily to retrieve it.

"Stupid… Who throws a fucking gun?"

"Who HAS a fucking gun?! You're a….what? Terrorist? Criminal?" frustration stopped her ranting, stalling her ability to find words. Sasha stared daggers at him.

Col shook his head and tried to calm his breathing before beginning an explanation. As he was about to talk, he noticed someone in the distance behind Sasha. He flashed a look at his watch.

"What day is it?"

"Um, Thursday? Friday morning…."

"Shit! Come on" he grabbed her wrist and took off across the moorland back in the direction of his truck. Sasha, still wearing her slip, tried her best to keep up with him, but stumbled and grabbed her ankle, wincing in pain. Col collapsed around her.

“What?” he asked urgently

“You have longer legs than I do!” She cried.

Col looked up, over a large boulder that seemed to be protecting them from sight, and watched as a latino looking man approached his truck; peered through the windows and leaned back on the empty vehicle.

Juan pulled out his mobile and dialled, holding it up to his ear waiting for connection.

Col suddenly realised, and started searching through his clothing.

“Fucking hell” he was frustrated, as his phone started to ring, he hadn’t got to it before it rang.

Juan immediately heard the ring tone and looked in their direction. The uneven ground thankfully offered them some protection from his immediate line of site. Col figured they had about 2 minutes before the man reached them.

“Who are you?” She whispered as carefully as she could.

“HM Customs & Excise.” He whispered.

“Customs?” she almost shouted before he threw a hand over her mouth.

“Joint task force...” he explained as quickly as he could, raising his head to check Juan’s position whenever he felt was safe to do so “SOCA and…”another check “Interpol.”

"Interpol?" Sasha couldn't take it in. "So, you're some kind of James Bond?!" She whispered incredulously.

It dawned on her that his Cornish accent had slipped further away. Col, in his true form, really did sound like James Bond – a muted down Scottish accent as though he'd had most of it beaten out of him at an English boarding school. She wondered how long he'd been keeping up the Cornish accent she'd become so familiar with. Col cocked his head trying to take in the description; until he noticed Juan getting too close for comfort.

"Don't you dare say a word" Col warned her, danger in his eyes. He grabbed her, pushed her down and started kissing her roughly, hands roaming all over her hungrily as though he wasn't about to give her any leeway to do anything she wanted to.

Sasha felt fear seething through her to her bones….this was feeling dangerously close to rape – had she not been so needful of him all the time and welcoming to any advances. That made this scarily exciting.

Suddenly, he stopped, left her in the state she was; emotionally and physically, now covered in mud and vegetation. He seemed unperturbed, stood up to his full height, oozing confidence, danger, and a dark, guarded expression hovering over his face.

Sasha opened her mouth to call his name, he glanced down and stood on her wrist, hard enough to give her a start, and a prominent red mark to have to try and explain away. She knew this was a further warning to stay quiet.

Juan approached Col and nodded a greeting, looking at the taller man suspiciously. Col grinned, a dangerous grin, shrugged by way of some kind of explanation, indicating Sasha, cleavage heaving and frightened expression on her face, crouching on the ground. Juan's sleazy face broke into a broad, understanding smile.

"Sorry for missing your call, pal. Was waiting in the car. Got a bit carried away." Col explained.

"No problem." Juan agreed with a slimy smirk on his face, still eyeing Sasha with whatever immoral, frightening thoughts were running through his head.

"What happened with the shipment, Juan?" Col demanded coldly, threateningly. Juan looked at him and shrugged.

"Didn't come in"

"Oh I know very well it didn't come in. What the fuck happened to it? You confirmed it had left Panama."

"They had a change of plans. News of…difficulties. The Captain re-routed the couriers."

"Re-routed?" Col shouted accusingly "Rerouted where?"

"Nouhadibou."

"Fucking Africa? That'll take a week to get up here!"

“We’re all working with…contraints….my friend” Juan tried to calm Col down, trying his best to hide his fear of this foreboding, whilst also eyeing up Sasha even more sleazily. Juan raised his eyebrows at Col, indicating Sasha questioningly.

“Don’t worry about it, she don’t understand English.” Col quipped, casually.

Juan nodded knowingly, and grinned a shady smile at Sasha, who took all her remaining strength not to gag.

“It’s no problem, Tangye.”

“It will be, Juan, if you don’t keep me informed. I have people breathing down my neck on this.” Juan nodded and took leave of the two. Col stared after him expressionlessly. Juan turned a couple of times as he walked away towards the open field that doubled as a car park.

“He’s gonna suspect something…” Col muttered without turning to look at Sasha. He stepped back and grabbed her arm, as gently as he could, trying to make it look rough, for the benefit of Juan.

She stared into his eyes like a frightened child. How could he have dragged her in to this? Col closed his eyes in despair at her expression. Checking back at Juan, Col mouthed ‘Sorry’ to her before claiming her mouth roughly, and then turning and half dragging her towards the car.

They drove in silence back to Tregiffen. Once Col was

sure they were clear of Juan, he pulled over, without saying a word and retrieved Sasha's dress from the back of the truck and handed it back to her. She nodded a silent thank you and slipped it back on. Col started driving again. Sasha still couldn't get her head around his revelation.

He was talking. He was giving her technical information. She supposed. She wasn't following, but of course he couldn't give her certain information she guessed.

He was still, after all, supposed to be undercover. He was giving her everything he could to prove to her that this time, he was telling the truth.

Sasha heard only a blur, a cacophony of sound in the tone of his voice. She suddenly tuned in again. Col turned and looked at her. "Have you listened to ANYTHING?" he snapped. He shook his head.

"Sorry." She mumbled, still bemused from shock. Some of the things he was saying were starting to get through.

"Panama. We get word from overseas agents that a shipment has left, that they couldn't intercept. Sometimes it doesn't turn up in Liverpool, or wherever they've reported it's headed. Then some drug bust on the streets of London recovers the shipment, so it came in somehow."

"What, exactly?"

"Cannabis and Crack from the Caribbean. Some other stuff from Peru and Ecuador. There's a possibility they're handing it off offshore and using old smuggling routes into the South coast to get it in."

Sasha laughed. "Smuggling? In Cornwall? Of course!" she laughed incredulously, "So, you're the last line of defence?"

"I'm one of a few. Dotted around. Not just Cornwall, anywhere with exposed, uninhabited coastline, really."

They pulled up outside the 'Rest'. Neither of them moved initially. Sitting in the truck.

"Did you know you were supposed to meet him there? Tonight, I mean?"

"I think I got my days mixed up." Col shook his head apologetically then continued, "We went out on Thursday evening, remember? When I had his meeting arranged for Friday morning I didn't make the link. Besides, we got a little carried away – I wasn't expecting to …"

"Co-incidence you took me to the same place?" Sasha challenged.

"I was trying to think of an appropriate deserted place."

"For sex or for meeting smugglers?"

"Both I guess." He shrugged, remorsefully.

It was almost 4am. It had begun to rain again.

"I guess that's it then?" Sasha sighed. Col looked at her

questioningly. “I’m sorry, about saying … you know” she said, looking down.

“What?”

“I said ‘I love you’ and you…ran away”

Col caught on. He rolled his eyes and searched through his pockets.

“I went to get these.” He tossed a 3-pack of Durex onto the dash board. Sasha felt a lump rise in her throat, stopping her breathing momentarily.

“Oh” she said, finally.

Sasha got out of the car in a daze and headed for the pub. She fumbled for the key in the bottom of her bag, her head spinning. Col caught her before she collapsed completely, and held her up with one arm, he opened the door with his own key. Martha had given them each a key as guests so they could come and go as they pleased.

They stumbled in through the door. In the darkness of the pub, they heard the sound of the rain thundering on the window. Sasha head was buzzing with the night’s events.

So, he really didn’t mind that she had told him she loved him? But he was an undercover Customs officer? Had she really done those things in the back of the truck?

Pinned against the knotted, ancient, wood-beamed wall by her hands, Sasha closed her eyes and inhaled deeply. That strong stench that had first repelled her was penetrating her soul. The musky scent of him, merged with sweet apple cider and the strong tobacco, and that strange contrasting, confusing tinge that reminded her of freshly collected dry cleaning. At least this had been explained – he must have been checking in with superiors occasionally, getting stuff from home…wherever that was…

Colan's hands let go of hers and slid down her arms. She opened her eyes in surprise and found herself being stared at intensely. Not menacingly with hatred and danger; but with hunger, a needful passion that changed the mood completely.

There was loneliness, a void, in his expression that suddenly changed the large, rough beast in front of her once again into a lost, forlorn youth in need of someone. Not just someone, she thought, he was staring into her like he needed her.

Her mouth felt dry, her pulse quickened. Sasha swallowed to try and clear the lump from her throat as his hands ever so slowly continued moving down her torso, encircling her waist and pulling her away from the wall and towards him. He held her gaze the whole time, as though searching her mind through her eyes, somehow scared she would rebuff him. She felt his heartbeat, somehow quicker than hers, and the heat from him making her forget their desperation to start the fire for warmth. His head moved forwards, lowering his face towards hers.

Suddenly a desperate groan escaped his lips and instead

of the deep, long, passionate kiss she had been expecting, his eyes dropped and he buried his face in her neck. OK, no kiss, but, Oh Boy her senses were tingling.

He breathed into her neck, alternating kisses and licks around her throat. Colan seemed to be drinking in the scent of her as much as she had him. Her toes curled as he pulled the strap of her dress down off her shoulder and his head moved lower.

Sasha's head fell back. Her body was yearning for him to get on with it but she didn't want him to stop the tantalising path he was taking. Colan tugged at the other shoulder strap and pulled her slip down to her waist, revealing her bra. He grunted again, in what may have been appreciation, she couldn't be sure, and took her left breast in his hand, cupping it gently like it was some prize he'd never been allowed to touch.

He bent his head to kiss her nipple through the fabric and she breathed in the strong aroma of his glistening black hair, drying from the rain.

"Mm that's nice" she whispered, once again closing her eyes and rolling her head back, "Oh God, Col"

"Oh Sarah" he murmured into her chest as he began to move his attention to the right breast, and moved a hand up inside the back of her shirt with the intention of unhooking her bra.

Sasha froze for a moment, her breathing stalled. Her head snapped back upright and eyes wide open, staring down at the top of his head. Gathering herself, she pushed back at his shoulders to get him away from her.

The stunned fisherman stared back at her, with a gaze now filed with a dreaded realisation of what he'd said.

"Sarah?" Sasha stated, harshly.

Colan, within seconds, gathered himself together. His mouth, having been agape in shock, now lips pursed, he grabbed his coat and without any further sound or insight into his feelings, stalked out of the pub into the stormy morning as the sky grew ever lighter, leaving the heavy door wide open.

Sasha ran to the door after him. He was heading down to the quay, she thought. She was in two minds to follow him. As she watched him storm off, slinging his heavy jacket over him and pulling his hat down over his head, she felt the cold and the driving rain attacking her bared shoulders and thought the better of it.

Stepping back and closing the heavy door, Sasha fell back into one of the heavy, velvet covered pub chairs, trying to gather her thoughts, the threat of tears stinging behind her eyes once again.

15

The next thing Sasha knew, she woke up having dozed off in the chair. She knew she needed to see Colan at the first opportunity. There was no way she could let things lay the way they had gone earlier.

After everything she had been feeling; for him; about him; and the things he'd done to her, that couldn't be the end of it, surely? Panicked thoughts ran through her head.

Maybe "Sarah" was a mistake.

Maybe Sarah was the reason he'd gone undercover?

Sasha had no idea what to make of anything anymore; after jumping to whatever conclusions she had before his revelation. Rousing and finding it was almost 9.30, a sudden fright got hold of her.

Please don't let him have gone, she begged the powers that be, under her breath, Please.

Knowing full well, however, if the boat was going out, they should have left hours ago.

After running upstairs to take off her dress and petticoat and put something a little more practical on, she rushed down to the dockside in a mid-length skirt and an oversized t-shirt. The rain had not eased off; the sea looked rough as hell, even in this sheltered haven.

Her t-shirt was almost soaked through and her skirt whipped around her knees as she ran down the hill. From around the corner she couldn't see the mooring where "Claudia" usually was; but hoped against hope the crazy crew had decided it was too rough to go out today.

No such luck. Soaked through again, hair dripping into her eyes, she wasn't sure if tears were welling up in frustration at the site of the empty spot where the vessel usually was.

Ned appeared from the harbourmaster's hut, in full wet weather gear.

"They're gone they 'ave, if your lookin' for "Claudia""

"In this weather? " Sasha asked incredulously.

"Kinda normal for ol'George if you ask me. " Ned looked at her.

"Colan weren't there, if you're wonderin' " Sasha stared at him. Ned sometimes, especially now, seemed so much older than his years.

"He didn't turn out this mornin'and I ain't seen 'is truck neither. "

"OK. Thanks Ned." She forced a smile at him.

At a loss for what to do next, Sasha hid in the bus shelter

rather than return directly to the 'Rest'. Within a few minutes, the morning bus from Penzance started chugging down the hill towards her. In a split second decision she waved it down, fished some change from her pocket.

"Land's End please." The driver punched in the fare and rang out her ticket. She wobbled into the nearest seat as he moved off before even giving her a chance to get down the aisle. She had suddenly decided to just go for a walk. In the rain and the wind she decided didn't matter, in fact, made a bit of fresh air a bit more appealing – why shouldn't she go walking across wild scrubland in wild weather when her mood was as confused as it was.

The Land's End complex was pretty much deserted, the weather keeping the hordes of tourists away. Sasha saw the odd local walking their dogs across the open moorland, or following the coastal path up from Sennen Cove. She was stood on the rope bridge crossing a deep, wild gorge, staring out to sea, the wind and the rain whipping her face. Clinging on to the ropes, she could see the wreck of Mulheim quite clearly from here. She was compelled to walk along towards it and get a closer look. It looked more fascinating and eerie in this weather. The cold grey skies and the waves roughly washing over the remains. It made for a very sad and lonely sight, matching Sasha's mood.

Who was Sarah? Was she the reason he'd accepted an undercover role? The more she thought about it the more the realisation struck her she knew even less about him now she knew what he was.

Before, she'd known he was Cornish, she'd known he was a fisherman, she'd known who his friends and colleagues were; she'd known he was single…

Oh Goodness…what if, like when she'd been questioned by Leigh, he's not single in his real life?

What if, once this was over, he'd go back to his Sarah, in their cosy semi and 2.4 children?

Would he laugh down the pub with his mates about the characters he'd met in Cornwall? Would she be one?

Sasha thought back to the early hours of the morning and the meeting with Juan – she'd been a good cover for Col's forgetfulness – Juan had accepted it wholeheartedly that Col was just chasing a bit of skirt while waiting for more important things…

What if this was his plan all along? She was part of this cover? Interwoven into the fake life he was hiding in? Stupid, Stupid girl! She chastised herself. I considered moving here to be with him!

But how DARE he let me believe it? She wasn't sure if she should be angrier at him or with herself for almost ruining her life for him. Sasha continued walking along the coast path, down towards Sennen, her mind racing and her body feeling in a state of sunken despair.

After everything, it had all been just sex. Physical attraction, sex and probably just down to frustration on his part – if he'd been alone for 3 years and the village being so small, she was obvious fodder – coming in for a visit and leaving after a short time. Perfect for a bit of fun with no strings attached. Perfect for his role.

When Sasha arrived down at Sennen, she'd been walking for a good couple of hours, not strictly sticking to the path. She didn't feel like heading back to Tregiffen yet; she kept waking, aimlessly; climbing the steep hill out of the cove to the rest of Sennen, up on the main road. She'd seen a pub up next to the old church. Maybe a quiet drink in a dark place, out of the weather, would clear her head a little.

16

Col had driven away wishing he could forget about what he just did. Idiot. Nothing a woman hates worse than being called another woman's name. As if it wasn't bad enough using her the way he had to cover himself with Juan; all the confusing ways he'd acted towards her up until now.

He kept driving; hoping time would pass quickly until his rendezvous with Juan and his boys that afternoon. At least on the work front, things were looking up.

He had spent the past 3 years ingraining himself into life as a Cornish fisherman, talking to the wrong people in the wrong places in pubs and bars and on docks at night from Newlyn to Falmouth and everywhere in between.

He'd got in good with a man who knew a South American named Juan, who lived in Penzance and apparently worked delivering cars around the country for an executive car company.

Describing Juan to his superiors, they became very interested. This man fitted a description they already had; and a job like that would not raise any suspicion if he were to move contraband from a landing site in the middle of the night to anywhere in the UK; or even to mainland Europe.

Trying to come up with a way of approaching him, without the desperation of a junkie, Col had managed to get him talking, suggesting he had a few friends who would be interested in purchasing some of his wares.

He had to appear important enough for Juan to be happy to share some of the product with him, but not so confident that he was a key player – if Juan dug too much into his background he'd be dead.

A fisherman, with a side line and some reliable clients, that was enough. So far he'd managed to secure a few small samples from Juan.

Colan had gotten them back to HQ and they'd confirmed it was the stuff they'd been looking for – shipments from Panama, where they had an agent based, who informed them whenever a shipment was on its way, if they could.

The trick now, was catching the shipments coming ashore – when, where, how; He may have had enough to get Juan on possession but without catching the others in the act or putting a stop to their routes.

Col had a feeling Juan would let something slip today, after the missing shipment, and he thought he may have put on enough of a show of menace at his displeasure to the smaller man, that Juan may try and get him more involved by way of an apology, to keep him happy.

But not if he was distracted. Not if he was thinking about Sasha and everything they'd been through, only for him to go and do a stupid thing like…

His phone vibrated on the passenger seat next to him. The screen lit up with a text message. He was hoping against hope it would be Sasha wanting to see him.

'Report on Juan Mendez available. Call in for info.'

Drat. He threw the phone back onto the seat. He checked his watch – almost time to meet with Juan near Lizard Point.

17

Juan hated the British weather. This rain was one thing but the wind and the sheer dreariness of the whole sky. And all the time… no distinct seasons. He was getting tired of being here.

He needed to get back. But there was still a lot of money to be made. A lot of desperate people who would find money to give him, in return for what only he could get.

He was stood above a small, discreet cove, planning the evening's landing. His job was being made ever easier in this part of the world – Fewer authorities to patrol the wild Cornish coastline meant he hardly had to bother looking over his shoulder. However it had been brought to his attention by his network that more often than not these days, shipments would be seized upon delivery after they'd been through his hands; even though they were successfully clearing the ships before they got to Liverpool, HM Customs up there were tirelessly searching each ship with a fine tooth comb. His network knew the ships were being earmarked on purpose – information was being sent on. They suspected a few people on shore in Panama; others on some of the vessels.

So far there had been no notion that their smaller fleet of boats – usually fishing boats manned by his men, older boats, blending in with the old-fashioned and laid-back Cornish landscape – had been heading out to sea and liaising with the ships, taking the merchandise on board and bringing it back in to somewhere along the Cornish coast previously agreed with Juan, where there was no Customs presence to speak of.

So, somehow, information was getting to the UK authorities that the goods were present at his dealers' homes – they were coming to know that the stuff was there before it had a chance to get to the streets. It was only a matter of time before they began to trace back and try and seize it at source – him and his boats, as it came ashore.

Recently, he'd been switching the landing sites more and more often to keep ahead of the game. In the meantime, he'd had some background checks done on some people around him. He'd not got much info back on Colan Tangye, but what was strange was they could find no information on him prior to three years ago when he signed on to work on a fishing vessel out of Tregiffen. It was highly unusual to appear out of nowhere. Everyone has a past – especially someone who knows the type of people who want what Juan had to offer.

Maybe it was about time to push Col Tangye a little further, to see if he breaks. In the interests of fairness, Juan was also interested to know a bit more about the woman Col had been with the other night.

For one thing, she could know a bit more about Col – information Juan would be most interested in; for another, she intrigued him a little. If she was nothing more than a passing fancy in Col's life, maybe she would be available to spend a little time with Juan.

That was, unless she was paid by the hour and Col could pass on some contact details.

He had his men on the lookout for her in any case. Col's truck pulled up, dead on time, Juan noticed, glancing at his watch. Juan stood still as Col jumped down from his vehicle. Juan watched and waited as the larger man approached him.

Looking behind Col, he made sure his companion, a large, almost sumo-statured creature, took up a position behind Col, between him and his vehicle.

"So, you got some news, Juan?"

"I do, yes. We have a new location, as you can see." Outside of Col's view, the large man reached through the open window and grabbed his phone he'd left on the passenger seat.

"Good choice" Col agreed, looking down into the small cove, well enclosed and out of view of any buildings, with a clear stretch of sand, it would be easy enough to get a small boat on and off the beach without too much hassle from jutting rocks.

"This one has a nice cave system, we've recently discovered. Helps keep us out of view, you see" Juan explained to Col; giving him reassurance that the man was finally about to take him into his confidence.

"Sounds good. Did you manage to get another shipment in this week?"

"Tonight, as it happens." Juan shrugged "It's just a shame I've had to change locations on the boys so often – makes the treacherous coastal conditions a little more dangerous than it needs to be, lack of familiarity on the part of the crew."

"Yeah, well, I know all about being at sea. How's it going with the moving – you managing to stay under the radar I see?"

Col's excitement was building… a shipment tonight? Maybe he'd finally be able to bring this gang's actions to an end and get out of here. Take Sasha by the hand and run and begin something new together…

Sumo tossed Col's phone to Juan, having checked the screen. He nodded at Juan.

"Under the radar by being very, very careful about those with which we do business…" Col's heart sank. Without betraying himself with his expression; he recognised the phone that had just been thrown as being his own. He glanced back at the Sumo guy standing between him and his truck.

Shit… he hadn't deleted the message. What's more, it was still up on the screen. He'd been too busy thinking about Sasha to ensure he deleted his messages.

"Interesting that someone like you, in your position, would need a 'report on Juan Mendez', don't you think my friend?" Juan's demeanour gave nothing away. He remained calm and reflective. He barely looked in Col's direction, preferring to keep viewing the cove below them.

"Who shall we be calling in to, then, Mr Tangye?" Juan turned to him, and cocked his head to beckon for Sumo to come and search Col. Col had no answer to this. He realised he was trapped, as the large man pulled this gun out from under his coat, handing it to Juan.

He could fight. No doubt he could knock out Juan with one strike but he'd never seen this other man before; he had no idea if he could fight; besides he knew his own gun at least was loaded, there was no telling what other weaponry was around.

Juan nodded at the thug, who without much resistance zip-tied Col's hands behind his back and led him over to Col's truck. He bundled him in and fished the keys out of Col's pocket. Juan paused for a moment, alone on the cliff top.

Juan then fished his own phone from deep in his coat pocket, and set about making a call. Another one of his men should be set and poised to complete another part of his damage control, had Col turned out to be what he thought. He held the phone up to his ear.

"hello?' "Do it." Juan said, and hung up.

Juan nodded at Sumo who pushed Col from behind,

forcefully suggesting he start walking towards the cove. They passed Juan, smirking at Col as he passed. Juan shook his head and raised his eyebrows, and followed them down the narrow cliff face path.

18

Sasha had been sitting in a corner table in The First & Last, staring at the rain streaking down the windows, for goodness knows how long. She was so lost in thought she didn't even know what her own thoughts were any more.

She'd tried being a little social and chatted at the bar to a couple of old guys who seemed to be so local they held up the bar. Ancient mariners, retired to sit and recount tales of any random old thing to anyone who would listen.

After a while though, even after 2 ciders, Sasha couldn't concentrate, and took her leave of them, via the ladies, thinking it would seem a little more polite an excuse to leave them.

When she returned from the toilets, they had delved into a deep discussion of their own so she felt comfortable enough to not have to join them. The rest of the place was practically deserted, so she had her choice of tables. The one by the window had seemed most appropriate, misery loved company so the unhappy weather enticed her to be near one of the small windows.

After her third pint of cider, she wasn't feeling too steady on her feet; and decided since she was there alone, the only way of getting back to Tregiffen would be bus or a rather long walk. Now was not a moment to be getting blind drunk.

She shakily returned her glass to the bar and smiled a thank you to the bar man. Exiting onto the main road, the driving rain was harder now and smacked her in the face. Wow that's one hell of a wake up, she thought.

She looked up and down the road, before deciding to head back down towards Land's End and pick the bus up there.

About 100 yards down the road, Sasha became aware a car was almost curb-crawling her, pulled up alongside her and wound the window down. This was no-one she recognised. Not an old man, maybe her age – late 20s? But he looked rough; sunken eyes, cigarette hanging out of his mouth, shaved crew-cut hairstyle below a filthy baseball cap; and he, or at least, the interior of the vehicle, stank to high heaven.

"How you doin'Sasha? " He asked.

Do I know him? Her mind tried to think back to the locals at the 'Rest'; surely he wasn't one of them? He wasn't anything to do with Ol'George's crew…maybe someone she'd been briefly introduced to at the Lifeboat fundraiser? After her karaoke stint no doubt she had made more of a memorable impression on them than they had on her. Not that she was trying to be rude but being introduced so quickly to so many people in such a short amount of time, given that she was so distracted by Col at the same time, it was hard to remember names and faces…

“Bit wet!” She admitted.

No harm in being friendly. Sure I’ll recognise him in a minute.

“Tell ya what, you need a lift? I saw Col earlier, looked a bit down, could take ya to him?”

Sasha’s spirits soared at the mention of Col’s name, combined with 3 pints of cider on an empty stomach; she saw nothing wrong with taking advantage of the good fortune of a lift.

Well, if this guy knows him…people are so friendly down here! Must be from the lifeboat social the other night. Yes, that was it.

Sasha was talking herself into it. She was sure now she had seen this guy at the makeshift bar with Sandy at one point. Sasha opened the door and climbed in, momentarily relieved to be out of the weather.

The guy sniggered. How fucking easy was that? He considered talking to her the whole way there, but not taking any chances, he stuck to what Juan had told him.

Grab her, incapacitate her, and get her here. Swift of hand, he grabbed the prepared chloroform handkerchief he had hidden down beside his seat and held it over her mouth. Sasha slumped forward in the passenger seat. He revved the engine and sped away.

19

“Stupid Cow. Mum never tell ya to not get into cars with strangers?” Col chided.

Coming round, she found him holding her head close to his chest and wiping her forehead. She felt cold, and whatever her knee-jerk reaction to waking to find Col there, she was glad of the closeness for no other reason than the sharing of body heat.

“What? Where…” She looked around, confused.

A cave? They were in a cave. Not just an empty cavern like she’d been in on adventure trips and outward bound courses, this one looked like something out of an old fashioned pirate movie.

She tried to focus, crates lining the walls?

“Wow it looks like a set from a Smuggling movie…” Col raised her eyebrows at her.

“Oh….smuggling…” Finally, she’d caught on. Or…maybe not... Her eyes were coming around to the darkness, and there was a naked bulb attached to a fitting, being powered by a cable snaking away out of sight further down the passageway.

“How did you find me?” She asked him.

“I didn’t find you. Juan caught on. About me. Three years fucking hard work and he gets it from a text message”

“A text message? I don’t understand…what’s going on? Where are we?” Sasha was getting more worried by the moment.

Forget about falling unconscious and waking up here – she had been relieved to see Col when she came round, but the more she came round, reality was hitting her square in the face.

“I had a meet arranged with Juan. It was a bit of an ambush to be honest. I wasn’t paying attention. Next thing I know they’ve brought me here. Entrance is currently blocked and guarded. Don’t worry, I’ve tried.” He said as she began to look around for another way out. “An hour or so later they brought you in, dumped you on the ground laughing.”

Sasha covered her face with her hands.

“I’d had a couple of drinks. I thought I recognised him.”

Col tried to comfort her, a little “Listen they were out to get you. Whether you’d got in voluntarily or not, you wouldn’t have been able to fight them off. We’ve both been a little…distracted recently.”

“You don’t know that!” Col glanced at her. “OK.

Smugglers, I get it. I don't get what's in these boxes though – I thought drugs came in small packets, in baggies and hidden in people's shorts…"

"They're empty. I think, though, they've branched out. These didn't all have drugs in them. Some may have - bolder, braver shipments. I think they might be bringing in weapons via the same route."

Sasha's eyes widened "Weapons?"

"Oh not all from here, certain street gangs would be in the market in the big cities. A gateway to mainland Europe; and beyond. Exploiting the ease of passage they think they have here."

"What am I doing here?" Sasha questioned, uncertain if it was a valid question for Col, or kicking herself for allowing herself to get involved.

"I was trying to figure that out. I've been trying to protect you from this. Either Juan thinks you're working with me, after catching us together the other night; or else if he gets rid of me and there's someone running around looking for me asking questions, that'll bring in the authorities a lot earlier than he can deal with."

"So, what now?" Sasha asked.

"Now they kill us." Col said, honestly, sadly.

Sasha froze. Suddenly the stark reality of the situation hit her. He looked at her, then walked towards her and held her hands firmly in his, facing her.

“Sasha they’re drug smugglers. They’re in this for a lot of money. They’re not people smugglers or hostage takers or standing for any kind of noble cause. People get in the way. They’ll kill us, get us out of the way and get on with it.” “But..George…and Ned and everyone in Tregiffen?” Sasha couldn’t help but start to worry for other people, since their own situation seemed so hopeless she was trying to not think about it.

“They’ll not wipe out a whole village.” Col shook his head, “They’ll create some cover, a notice to say I’ve been arrested, or something; a train ticket stub suggesting you’ve returned home.”

“Someone will look for you…us…eventually? My boss if I don’t turn up at work, your boss…”

“I suspect that’s why we’re still alive. He’s probably after some way of getting rid of us they can get away with, giving them enough time to pack up and move operations.”

She stumbled backwards a little and sat down on a rock shelf jutting out from the wall. She sat as still as possible, but couldn’t hide the shaking that was taking over her. She didn’t think it was the cold any more.

Too shocked to cry and trying to hide the fear anyway, she couldn’t hide it from him. Col kneeled down on the cold, muddy ground in front of the rock she was perched on and once again, put a hand either side of her, this time holding her arms, just below her shoulders.

“I tried. Believe me I tried so hard to avoid you.”

“You could have said….something….”

“You think any conversation between us would have convinced either of us to stay away?” He chided, “I was over the moon when you ran away after the first night – you were out of any danger, away from me.”

“You’re a liar.” Sasha stared at him, involuntary hatred in her eyes.

“No….”

“Yes. You’ve been lying for so long you don’t know any more. Now it’s just good lies and bad lies, but all lies….George, Ned, everyone in town … me…”

“It’s my job!” he exclaimed, almost with tears welling up in his eyes with the frustration.

“No-body’s forcing you.” She cried.

Col sighed, “Well, that’s debateable.”

“How can it be debateable? You chose your job?”

“Covert ops, undercover, stuff like this is, well they give you the option. Full work up on how it means cutting off from everyone and everything you know, at least for a certain duration.”

“So, you chose…” Sasha began.

He cut her off “I chose to… leave a painful memory behind.”

Sasha came around, a little, to understanding what he was getting at.

"Sarah?" She asked.

Col avoided her gaze and pursed his lips and stayed silent.

"So some ex-girlfriend does …something, you're still in love with her, decide to run and hide in your work then find someone to pretend she's her…"

"You are nothing like that bitch…" Sasha was stunned – I was NOT expecting THAT.

Col rolled his eyes, sighed deeply and pulled himself up to sit next to Sasha on the rock, so that he wasn't facing her and could talk without accusing eyes penetrating his soul during his explanation.

"I was a little in lust with her, I think. We were never … anything. Not really. We worked together. We did a couple of these covert things before and she really wound me up, crazy woman."

"Not an ex-girlfriend you want back? That I'm a replacement for?"

"She accused me of sexual harassment and almost got me fired. I never touched her." Sasha looked at him. He was clearly trying not to drudge up too many memories for himself, but still trying to be honest with her, give her the truth.

"So…why call me by her name?" Sasha threw her hands

up in exasperation.

Col shook his head.

"I've been kicking myself to try and figure out why. I don't know Sash, she was the last woman of any kind in my life, she's been tormenting me since I met you – because of her I took this job to get away, because of her … I don't know why I said her name – it was so… you….just you, there in front of me." He shifted again, moving around in front of her, taking her hands and looked up at her. "Sasha, I promise you, there was no way I was thinking of her."

Sasha couldn't decide what to believe. But in this dark, cold place, Col kneeling in front of her staring at her, desperate, in this weirdest of all situations, for her understanding, forgiveness, whatever, when they, he had told her, were about to die. Col gave up staring, gave up waiting for a response. He stood up and began searching around frantically for anything that would help them get out.

"I realised, I can't even say now if I love you….or not…"Sasha suggested.

"What does that mean?" He wasn't sure he understood what she was trying to say.

"I mean….I get so horny when you're around…" Col was caught off guard at her frankness. "Sorry; just trying to make a point. But, I fancy you, yes; you're perfect, amazing sex, right." Sasha shrugged, and continued fast talking as though trying to talk herself out of a situation.

Or trying to persuade herself away from her declaration of love the night before.

"But I thought I was falling for a gruff, uncomplicated fisherman with nothing....OK very little...to hide." She carried on, "I thought if I was going to move to be with you I'd be moving to a quaint fishing village in Cornwall and live like a fish wife with flour on my pinny from baking, watching out the window dreamily every morning for you to come home to me safely."

She sniffed a little, unsure if this was as a result of the drug they'd used to knock her out, or the cold, damp atmosphere in here, or whether she'd actually been crying. She continued, "Now, I don't know what to imagine."

"Nothing like living in the moment then?!"Col exclaimed.

He stopped for a moment, his head cocked to one side, staring at her. He moved forward and sat next to her again.

"I have a very basic 3-bed semi, in Surbiton. It's nice, hardly a castle but it's mine. I have a mortgage; parents, Ron & Mary in Reading and a sister in Oxshott – Nina, she married well and has 2 kids. I have worked for customs since leaving college and have pretty much worked my way up. I don't do undercover work all the time. I'd have probably been sat behind a desk as soon as this was all over."

"And telling me this is supposed to make me love you?"

Sasha was at a loss for anything else to respond with.

“Sash, I think you already do.” He whispered to her, taking her in his arms and kissing her head “You just over-think things.”

“But…”

“Look, it was me who took you to St Just and Newlyn and we had a blast; it was me you were with at the lifeboat social; you’re right, the sex is amazing but that’s only part of it. Every moment we’ve spent together I’ve been myself. Maybe apart from when we first met, on the quay.”

Sasha was once again melting. It was freezing in this cave, the cold and damp had been seeping into her clothes but now being held by him once again she forgot all about that. The overwhelming urge to feel Col inside her was mounting. She rubbed a hand across his chest, and whispered to him,

“How much are they paying attention? “

“Who?” he asked

“The guards at the entrance.”

“Not so much…but enough that we won’t get past them…”

Sasha silenced him with a kiss. Not soft and suggestive, this was urgent, needful, she found some amazing strength from somewhere to push him further and further back into the cage.

He struggled with taking his shirt off as she did the same, between kissing and pushing and groaning. Eventually, they found the end of the cave system – a rock fall must have closed off the tunnel a long time ago. Mounted on the cold, damp rocks at the back of a dark, musty cave, Sasha undid his flies allowing his trousers to fall to the ground, pulled down his boxers and lifted up her skirt, she manoeuvred them both so she could mount him properly. They began moving in accord; as though everything they had practiced had been leading up to this one union. This was urgency, she thought. No playing around or tantalising, just get to the point – a need to connect with him one more time before…

Sasha bent her head down and muffled her moan in his shoulder as she came; then lifted her head and stared into his eyes as much as they could see in the dark, as an determination built in his movements, a few erotic seconds later, he came, she saw it and stifled his groan with her mouth over his once again. Bathed in sweat, they collapsed to the earthy ground breathing heavily, both scared to let go, in case it was the last time.

"Sasha," Col whispered in the darkness.

"Mmmm?"

"I love you."

20

They lay there for what seemed like an age before movement could be heard at the entrance to the cave. Four or five burly men started searching around the main cavern, shouting in some unidentifiable language, muffled by the echoes and the darkness.

It was clear they were looking for Col and Sasha. The lovers dressed quickly and grabbed hold of each other as the men found them and dragged them out.

The sky was black and the stars out again, they must have been sat in each other's arms in the dark for hours. Juan was outside, overseeing the operation.

To Col's surprise there were two boats there, rather than just the one he had assumed was meeting the container ships out in the ocean to be handed the contraband.

Sasha and Col's faces fell. They were both were concerned to notice the second boat was "Claudia".

Sasha shot a frightened look at Col. What if George and the crew have been dragged into this as well? George, at the very least, would not cope with this, she thought. Whether Juan followed their train of thought or not, he seemed to feel the need to explain a little.

Sasha for some reason, maybe her brain was trying to find any light in the situation, couldn't help but think of countless "villain speeches" from comic books and movie adaptations – why do they always feel the need to give a farewell speech – dragging out the inevitable… …or giving the hero more time to figure out an escape?

She glanced sideways at Col, in case he showed some signs of a plan forming. Or…maybe not. Not a glimmer crossed his face.

"We have borrowed a vessel from some friends of yours. Don't worry, they are oblivious. We are aware the other members of the crew are innocent and we have no need to dispose of more people than absolutely necessary – it just creates more work for us to cover up."

"They're going to look for us though?" Sasha moaned, before her, or Col, could stop herself.

Col shook his head, suddenly following Juan's trail of thought.

"No, I'm afraid not," Juan corrected her "You see, your boyfriend here has been trying so hard to impress you; he decided to take his boss's boat out of an evening to treat you to a romantic cruise." Sasha and Col were simultaneously manhandled and pushed, and forced to climb aboard "Claudia".

"Unfortunate for him, his lack of experience of sailing alone at night around these cliffs and in rough weather;

coupled with his distraction of having a lover on board, led to an unfortunate incident at sea. All hands lost, we shall no doubt hear." Sasha understood completely.

"Boating accident?" she whispered miserably to Col as they were stiffly tied together in the cabin. He twisted his head round to meet her gaze, sadly. Three more of Juan's men climbed aboard "Claudia" and prepared to leave the cove.

For half an hour Sasha and Col sat in silence, each contemplating what was going to happen to them. Sasha, for one, felt some kind of weird comfort in the pit of her despair that if there was anyone she was with for what was about to happen, it was this man she had so recently fallen for.

Col, on the other hand, wasn't about to be beaten. He knew this boat like the back of his hand. He knew, for example, there was a sharp nick in the bow which he had used a few times to help him tend the ropes…

"Come on" he whispered to Sasha. She looked at him questioningly as he dragged her towards the broken wood and started rubbing their binds against it.

"Where we gonna go?!"She urged.

"Dunno yet but having free hands is gonna be in our favour, don't you think?" It took another thirty minutes or so for them to rub through the ties.

When they were finally free and rubbing their wrists, Sasha felt a little strange, empty even. Col was there, right next to her but somehow, considering the fate awaiting them, whatever it was, up on deck, that didn't seem half close enough. Through the window they could see the sky beginning to lighten.

"They're gonna do it soon. Cover of darkness is good" Col mentioned as immediately one of the men came through the door. They were enough out of his line of site for their lack of binds not be immediately noticeable to him.

They nestled close to each other back in the position they had been tied. He didn't look at them immediately. He set about setting some explosives in the cabin, wiring around the side. Sasha swallowed hard and began to feel a bit feint.

Col must've been aware of her fear – he grabbed her hand and squeezed hard, turning his head to kiss her on top of her head.

"One less of them should be easier to handle." He whispered to Sasha.

Suddenly, when the man's back was turned, Col grabbed him around the neck from behind and hit him deftly, swiftly, making Sasha jump, and swoon slightly that this was…kind of… her man.

He grabbed her hand and pulled her towards the door. He could see the other two on deck. One was tossing lines to the other boat – the smaller one that had been on the beach with "Claudia"; probably, he surmised, in preparation for them making an escape, once they'd set

Claudia to blow.

Col moved back from the door and looked Sasha in the eye. “Sash, the only way we’re gonna get out of this is by gettin’ very, very wet. I recon I can take those two if I get ‘em by surprise but only one of these boats is getting away from here – I don’t think once they set these explosives I’m gonna be able to stop ‘em. We’re not gonna be able to get over to the other boat without being in a clear line of fire. We have to assume they have guns. They definitely have mine at least.”

“But we’ve been moving for ages – we can’t swim to shore? “ Sasha was on the verge of panic now.

“No, but if I can get to the radio before we blow I can at least send out a mayday and report our position.”

“So?”

“So… I want you to scream. We need to get those two out of the way without the other boat suspecting immediately.”

“Scream?”

“Like you’re about to get raped.” He said succinctly. She stared at him.

“Not by me…by him!” He corrected, pointing at the unconscious guy on the floor. Sasha actually felt a little disappointed…she had to admit that against her better judgement, a rape fantasy with Col was kinda getting her aroused.

"When? Now?"

"Hang on..." He stopped her, and searched the unconscious thug on the floor for a weapon. No gun, unfortunately, but a knife at least.

"OK." He nodded at her and took a position behind the door.

"Wait..." He stopped her, just before she went ahead with her shout. He reached forward and ripped the shoulder of her t-shirt exposing her bra. She raised her eyebrows at him. He shrugged and winked, checked the door again and nodded.

Sasha let out a blood curdling scream.

Col, both impressed and terrified simultaneously, could see from his position the two men on deck look in the direction of the cabin. One cocked his head indicating to the other to go and check.

As he entered the cabin, he saw Sasha crouching in the back facing him, breathing heavy and faltering. He glanced at his colleague on the floor then back at Sasha, before being hit quite squarely over the head by Col from behind.

Outside, although it was getting light, the rain was lashing down and the sea getting rougher by the minute. Before the last thug on board "Claudia" , and subsequently the others on the other boat, noticed the kerfuffle in the cabin, Col pulled Sasha to him.

“The sea is going to be rough. Don’t try and hold on if we get separated. You can’t fight the current. Currents are too strong. You have two choices, let it take you, or go with it. Relax, don’t fight, it’ll save your energy.”

It took Sasha a moment to realise the gravitas of what he was saying. She looked at him with growing horror in her eyes. He drew her to him and kissed her deeply again, breathing her in and pressing his chest up against her.

“We’re going to try and make it to the radio up top.”

“Can’t I stay in here?” she pleaded. Col shook his head firmly.

“If you get stuck in here you have no hope – you’ll go down with the ship. You stay close to me.” He looked around, and stripped the thick leather jacket off the second accomplice on the floor and made her put it on.

“It’ll protect you a little, I hope, from…whatever. When you hit the water try and take it off.”

“But…”

“It won’t keep you warm in the water; it’ll just drag you down. Ready? “

She nodded. He grabbed her hand and they sneaked as stealthily as they could from the cabin door up to the cockpit where the radio was. He scribbled down the co-ordinates from the GPS on deck and pointed to the radio to Sasha.

She didn't quite understand, but he cocked his head towards the third man still fussing securing the rope between them and the other boat, and fiddling with the buoys along the side, the increasingly rough seas making it treacherous to have the two boats so close together.

Sasha grabbed the radio handset from Col's hand as he held it out to her.

Before he could turn on the third man, the target had already noticed them.

He pulled a gun and shot Col in the arm.

Sasha screamed again. Col jumped over towards the man and began wrestling with him.

"Sasha!" he shouted

She took that as her cue and began calling into the radio handset, pressing the button. "Mayday, Mayday! Help! Is there anyone there?"

She looked blankly at the radio. She wondered if it was on the right channel. It was definitely on. Why the hell didn't he tell me how to work it first? She used radios at the airport all the time, but had no idea if the terminology would be the same; and this was a different model from what she was used to.

"Hello? Claudia?" the radio crackled into life "Help! Coastguard!" Oh thank God, she thought.

As Sasha shouted as much information as she could into the radio as clearly as she could in her panic, Col watched through punches and struggles to keep the man's gun pointed away from her.

He glanced at his own shoulder as he wrestled; barely a graze, luckily. Suddenly shouts came from the other boat and another bullet whizzed past him, straight into the radio Sasha was talking to.

She screamed and hit the deck, eyes closed tightly, trying to grip anything for dear life. Col found a surge of strength from somewhere and hit the thug one more time, just enough in the right place to knock him down and give him enough time to run, grab Sasha, pull her up and throw themselves from "Claudia", into the choppy seas below.

"Swim!" He ordered her, and they struggled their way away from the vessels as fast as they could. Bullets whizzed towards them.

"Remember what I said! About the current!" Col spluttered trying to keep hold of her.

"Boats!" she shouted, Col shook his head, just as Claudia exploded. The other boat, still attached to the rope, had three panicking sailors aboard trying their best to shoot at the rope to detach it. They succeeded and moved away from the burning wreckage of "Claudia" as fast as they could.

They shouted to each other pointing in Col and Sasha's direction; one of them shot towards them before they gave up and took off. As they disappeared into the rapidly lightening horizon, the waves grew bigger. Sasha grabbed for Col's arm and screamed in panic as she saw blood swirling around the surface.

"Oh my God!" She shouted, flailing around looking at her own arms and as much of herself as she could in the water to find out where the blood was coming from.

"I think I've been hit again" he managed, his face growing a pale grey, looking as though his strength was waning.

Knowing she was going to have to be strong for both of them, Sasha struggled and managed to remove both the heavy jacket Col had put on her and her skirt, before becoming overcome by the waves. She was tossed around in the swells for what felt like an age, when she finally surfaced she couldn't see Col anywhere.

She shouted for him, and became aware that she was crying, out loud, alone. It could have been minutes, hours or longer, before she found herself looking up.

She could have sworn she heard a helicopter, although with the rain hammering on the roaring waters around her it could have been anything.

"Claudia" had all but disappeared beneath the waves, but she found herself clinging to one last remnant – part of the bow with the name emblazoned on it. Time passing was irrelevant to Sasha after that point.

She did come to realise, however, that the weather was calming a little as the Coastguard Search & Rescue helicopter hovered over her, motioning to her in her fatigue that they would hoist her up.

She should have felt relief, a gladness at being found, and by ‘the good guys’. All Sasha could feel was numb, both physically and emotionally. Because if she’d let any feeling in, her heart would be breaking.

21

It took Sasha a while in an emergency recovery room to come round from her exhausted, hypothermic state.

She was aware of an authoritative figure overseeing her recovery.

Martin King looked in on her every now and again, wrapped in her foil blanket and hooked up to beeping machinery.

She must have dozed, because at one point she woke up, suddenly feeling a lot more awake. She was offered a cup of tea and helped to sit up. Her mind was swimming.

"It's OK, Tabitha, I'll do the debrief here" he told a woman in a suit, as he closed the door behind him and pulled up another chair opposite Sasha. He had a kind face but an air of authority. His voice was quiet, calm, soothing. Sasha knew she would have liked him, if she had let herself feel anything.

"My name is Martin King. I'm the acting head of Her Majesty's Customs for this area. Can you tell me your name?"

"Sasha Pender" she murmured with all her might, in a

tired drawl.

“Thank you Ms. Pender. We couldn’t find any identification on you.” He offered, by way of some kind of explanation.

Martin proceeded to explain to her how they had received a call from the coastguard regarding an operative of theirs. During the debrief process she felt as though she were in a daze, hearing her own voice as though it weren’t coming from her.

She heard herself recounting her experience to Martin, with maybe a little more information than was required interspersed into her tale, causing him to raise an eyebrow more than once.

At one point, nearing the end of her story, a young man wearing a white shirt with epaulettes entered the room and beckoned to Martin.

The older man excused himself and stood by the man at the door. They muttered quietly as though keeping information between them.

Martin listened carefully, nodded matter-of-factly, and after a pause, spoke. “OK. Call off Air & Sea Rescue in that case, and notify his family.”

“And the body?” the second man whispered.

“I’ll take a look when I’ve finished here”

Sasha’s heart sank. She stared out of the window. Wherever she was, the sky had cleared and the sun was shining again; as it had been for the week the first time she came.

“Right then, Ms Pender. We’ll be in touch if we need anything more from you. In the meantime, I’ll have someone take you back to the inn you were staying at to collect your belongings. I expect you’ll want to return to your family after your ordeal. I’ll have someone notify the Inn you’re on your way”

22

"Shame about the lad," sniffed old George.

Sasha entered the dark bar just as he spoke. He looked directly at her and stroked his beard.

"I weren't talking 'bout you, lass; he were a damned good fisherman; and strong too. Dunno what I'm going to do now. And that bloody boat too…"

"He wan't a fisherman, George," shouted Ned from along the bar, "He were like FBI or sumthin. Like on TV"

Martha rushed around to take Sasha by the arm.

"Don't you worry lass, I've got your stuff together. We thought you'd be wanting to get on a train as soon as possible. Jimmy'll drive you"

Sasha appreciated Martha's caring attitude all the more. "Did they…tell you what happened?" Sasha asked her, falteringly.

"About George's boat? 'Course. Well, they told George at least. Said you was bein' treated and they'd bring you back. Sorry state of affairs, eh?"

Sasha smiled sadly, and then made her way alone upstairs to her room. As Martha had promised, her bag was neatly packed on the bed, still open to show everything was in there smartly. When she was finally sure she had checked the room for everything and made her way back down stairs, the place was quiet, sombre.

Those present either averted their eyes or offered her a supportive smile. She was glad no-one wanted to talk. She wasn't in any mood or fit state to talk to anyone. Jimmy drove her to the train station in silence. When they pulled up in the car park, he told her to wait in the café, while he went to organize her ticket.

He came back, handed her a ticket for the next train.

"Leaves in 20 minutes" he muttered. He smiled comfortingly at her, then turned away from her, and headed for the counter.

After a while, he returned with a handful of food – pre-packed sandwiches, biscuits, and apple and a banana and a bag of crisps. He dropped them on the table.

"Shoulda asked for a bag" he muttered again and turned away to go back to the counter.

"Jimmy you don't …" she tried to stop him, but he'd already gone. He came back with a bottle of water, a cardboard cup of coffee and a paper bag; he proceeded to stuff the food and snacks into it.

"Jimmy you really didn't need to get this…I don't…." Sasha weakly started as she fumbled for her purse in her bag next to her.

Jimmy shook his head and put his hand over hers.

"Orders from Martha, make sure you're stocked up for the journey so you can just sit back and rest. Think she even charged up your little music box too if you check."

Sasha hadn't even thought, but in the front pocket of her bag she found her MP3 player, and the charger very neatly wrapped into itself and tied with a small elastic band.

She smiled to herself at the thought of Martha carefully winding the cord and being so motherly. Jimmy said little more, but walked her to the platform, and like a proper gentleman held her hand as she climbed aboard, kissing it lightly before letting it go. Sasha smiled a sad thank you at him and took a seat by the window.

The train pulled slowly from the station and Sasha spent most of the 5 hour journey with tears in her eyes, staring at the landscape that looked so different to her after all that had happened to her.

23

A month or so had passed since Sasha's return. She had taken a few days at home to recover and not really spoken to anyone.

She didn't bother going shopping either so avoiding the stale milk in the fridge meant drinking black tea and coffee, and very slothfully lived on fish and chips from the chippy round the corner.

She would have the TV on in front of her but never really followed what was going on.

She more often than not just slept where she was on the sofa, barely caring enough to head upstairs.

It had been a good few nights, at least, before nightmares about the sea and the rescues and blood swirling in the water subsided and the vivid sexual dreams returned.

This time, though, it always was very definitely Col there, holding her, stroking, caressing, and taking her to the brink of frenzy; so much so that she would wake up already in tears. If she kept dreaming like this she'd never get over him, forget him.

Not that she wanted to forget him, but life would never

get easier and she'd never move on.

After a week being back in work of her being sullen and quiet, Leigh had had enough.

"Will you bloody tell me what the hell is going on with you? Did you break up with the guy? Coz no break up is worth the mood you've been forcing on us!"

Sasha had agreed to go with Leigh to Landing Lights for a long night session after their last shift before 2 off, and spilled the whole story.

She was met with incredulity, silence and, finally, a simple "Blimey" from her friend.

"Can't we leave it at that now?" Sasha really didn't want to talk about it again. "OK." Leigh agreed, knowing full well she'd try her best, but would have to tell the girls something.

At very least she'd have to stop in on Olga in the baggage hall to let her know what had been going on with Sasha. After she'd calmed down a little, Leigh realised her place. If Sasha had ever needed a friend, it was now.

"I'm sorry, Sash."

"I still dream about him."

"Is that why you look knackered like you haven't slept at all every time you come in?"

"Must be. It's not like I'm not trying. All I ever do is

sleep these days. All I can bring myself to do, Sofa, Bed….wherever."

"You really are in a bad way. Have you told your mum?"

Sasha shrugged.

"Told her it was a holiday romance break up." Sasha stared into her drink, then continued.

"It's not even like it was a break up. I can't even shout at him and blame him and leave nasty messages on Facebook or text him or anything…"

"Weirdo," chided Leigh.

"You know what I mean, Leigh. He fucked up my life and left me like this, but if we'd just broken up I'd be able to at least plot some kind of revenge to make myself feel better. He's dead – pretty final."

"What about a funeral?"

"I don't know" Sasha shrugged.

"You don't know? But they're supposed to be excellent for closure"

"I never asked. I was kind of in a daze at the hospital. It wasn't till I got home I realised I didn't know anyone who knew him; not really, I wouldn't know who to contact to find out about a funeral. It's too late now; it's been almost 2 months. It's probably over and done with, with Sarah….his parents… and whoever else mourning him. I think he said he had a sister."

Leigh took off towards the bar and came back with a tray carrying 2 tequila shots each, along with lime and salt on a plate.

"What's that for?" Sasha raised her eyebrows.

"Proper night out called for. Starting here. With these…" Leigh led the way and quickly did the first shot "then Frenchy said the Karaoke guy is setting up; then since it's Thursday, 'Easy's' is open 'til 4am, and we're off tomorrow."

Sasha took a deep breath.

"Well," she paused, thinking… maybe alcohol would allow her to forget for a little while …"If we have to walk home from there I'm getting a kebab on the way"

"Done" Leigh laughed, their single-girl ritual returning to help her get her friend back on the right path.

"Before we get too wasted, though, Sash …" Leigh put her hand over Sasha's as it rested on the table "I am really sorry, love."

Sasha knew full well Leigh would let on at least some of her tale to everyone else. They'd already been speculating while she was away about the renewal in her love life. She did know that Leigh was sincere with the apology, though.

Leigh had lost people she cared about; and cottoned on that Sasha had begun to really care about this man before she had lost him.

In the weeks that followed, the dreams continued.

Eventually, Leigh was forced to sit Sasha down and made a suggestion to her.

“It’s not like admitting your crazy, Sasha.”

“Leigh, I can’t see a psychiatrist!” Sasha said, not believing the suggestion had been put forward.

She went, of course; Leigh was right; these dreams were beginning to affect her greatly and since Col was dead she saw no other way of dealing with it.

She couldn’t very well, as she told Leigh, look him up, ‘diss’ him on social media or send him mean texts, this wasn’t a breakup, she’d never dealt with this before.

The therapist didn’t seem to do much at first. She sat there, silently, as Sasha began to recount the whole tale, from September 11th onwards.

After a few sessions, Sasha realised the bland looking, middle aged woman didn’t really need to say anything. That’s not what she was there for. She had her friends at work for advice; and mindless chatter; and gossip.

Combined, Sasha slowly began to notice the effects of the psychiatrist sessions and her friends’ pep-talks and returning to nights out, working.

The dreams slowed down to every now and again, usually a night before a day off after she’d had a lonely glass (or three) of wine before dragging herself up to bed and having a damned good bawling session, because despite the rest of the time, when she could let herself get on effectively with ‘real life’, she missed him, and wished he was part of it.

24

It was November.

In 5 months, they had managed to get Sasha almost – not quite – back to her old self.

She wasn't quite eyeing up new flight deck crews or scouring the business class line at the British Airways check-in for Mr Right.

Leigh imagined it would still be a long while before she even picked up her vibrator, let alone started her usual flirting.

In the office, Leigh and Sasha were digging through the dusty old box of second-hand, dust-covered Christmas decorations Mina had dug out from the store-room, ready to decorate the check-ins.

"So, Cath and Cheryl were saying there's a new Superintendent at Immigration."

Leigh jumped up onto the radio counter in the CSA office and plugged her walkie-talkie back into the charging slot.

“Really? Kevin’s gone?” Sasha blinked incredulously, “Slowly the whole face of this place is changing. All the old gang will be gone soon.”

“Yeah, I know, right? And Kevin didn’t say a word to anyone! ” Leigh exclaimed.

“That’s not like him.” Sasha mused, “You’d have thought he’d have been talking about it for weeks before hand if he had planned to leave. Wonder what happened?” Sasha said.

“Yeah, I know. I hate to mention it to you, you know, after…but they did say this new guy was worth a look…Come and meet the Brussels with me, and we’ll have a nose.”

“Sounds good. What check-in we rostered for?”

“We’re not,” Leigh checked the roster on the wall “looks like they’ve got the new girls without airside passes doing all the rest of the check-ins today. Leaves us with meeting and boarding, and baggage. Yuk.” Because of the imminent station shut-down, a few of the summer staff had had their temporary contracts extended for a few months to cover; but since it was not a long-term prospect, the intricate background checks and reference process of applying for security clearance to be able to freely work airside had been set aside, and the temps remained as ‘front of house’ cover to free up the experienced staff for meeting and boarding and other airside duties.

“Baggage isn’t bad,” argued Sasha, “Well, at least, it

wasn't when Kevin was there"

Sasha felt a little down as they led the passengers from the inbound flight to the immigration hall, where passengers were led before collecting their luggage. They'd line up under their relevant sign depending on which passport the held and would be checked and stamped, if needed, into the country.

Kevin Montague was the flamboyant head of the Immigration contingent at the airport. Larger than life, receding hairline but full of life; and always good for a hug if any of them were feeling down.

The HM Immigration office was not far from the baggage office; where the passenger services agents, under the watchful gaze of Olga, the baggage services supervisor, would be stationed to deal with reporting and locating and repatriating missing luggage and log reports of damaged luggage for insurance claims.

Downtime in between flights meant long hours filing reports, lugging heavy found luggage off the belt and around to the HM Customs X-ray and storage room.

This could be a long, boring, lonely process, especially on night shifts when a lot of the airport was shut down.

Kevin would relocate whoever was on his shift over to the baggage office if any of the CSA's were there alone and start an impromptu 'party'(albeit without booze and all above board – he was, if nothing else, a stickler for his job) and tell people how they'll re-enact the party properly at his and his husband's place on the weekend.

Sasha smiled to herself at the memory of all the good times that he'd been involved in.

"Afternoon laydeees!" Kevin boomed at them from the office door as he oversaw his officers at their podiums processing the inbound passengers.

"KEVIN!" Leigh beamed at him as she followed the last passengers into the hall from the flight.

She herded the passengers into the correct passport queues and veered off to stand by Kevin, as Sasha joined them.

"The girls said there was a new Immigration boss," Sasha gushed at him, confused at his presence but at the same time relieved. "We thought you'd gone without saying goodbye!"

"Customs, girls!" Kevin corrected. It took him a mere moment to realise where the confusion lay. "Ah. Of course. You know what some of the newbies are like – takes them a while to get the difference between Immigration and Customs. And let me tell you, he's bloody easy on the eye. I recon he's after skirt, personally, but given half a chance I'd not say no." He winked at them. Had they not known him as well they might have blushed, but this was very much along the lines of Kevin's usual speech pattern.

"Kevin!" Leigh chided, with mock astonishment.

"Don't mind me, Leelee! Jason wouldn't mind – he'd probably be up for a threesome when he sees this one…."

"Ewww…Sorry Kev…"started Sasha "I have nothing against being gay but I'd rather not think…."

Sasha stopped mid-sentence as she caught sight of something, or someone, across the hall. Kevin followed her gaze.

"Aha, speak of the devil…." Kevin would have quite happily carried on talking but Leigh was yanked around the corner by a hyper-ventilating Sasha.

"What the…"Leigh gasped.

"Col! Customs. Colan…" Sasha was struggling to speak.

Leigh took a moment then cottoned on to her friend's shock.

"THE Colan? Fisherman Colan?"

Leigh peeped out from around the wall they were hiding behind, to the amusement of an Asian family stood patiently in the immigration queue.

Colan and the customs officers, who were perusing the incoming baggage load on the belt and the accompanying passengers, glanced briefly in her direction at the sound of the merriment of the passengers.

Leigh waved and nodded animatedly then slipped back around the corner. The customs team shook off her odd behaviour and turned back to watching the passengers and their luggage leaving the hall. Colan was deep in conversation with one of the other officers, still having the ropes explained to him.

"He's fucking gorgeous!" Leigh exclaimed in surprise.

"Thanks for that!" Sasha retorted and stormed off down the corridor.

Leigh realised her shock might have come across as not having believed Sasha during all their conversations about her attraction to him. Now she felt bad and wished she'd held her tongue.

Leigh held her thumb up to Pilar who had followed the next flight in and was stood in the corner of the immigration hall. Pilar shrugged and nodded. Looked as though she'd have to clear this flight alone for now.

Leigh caught up with Sasha outside the smoke hole, the small outside but walled area where the ramp staff and baggage handlers were allowed to smoke, away from buildings and enclosed areas but also away from aircraft and fuel tanks. Since there were turnarounds in progress, loading and offloading of baggage, and pushbacks that needed doing, the place was momentarily deserted.

"Sorry." Sasha apologized. "Short of smoking one myself I'll just passively inhale here for a minute."

"Don't mind me," Leigh comforted, "But, bloody hell Sash, I don't blame you for getting in a tiz…"

The girls scrambled for their ear plugs as a 747 taxied past and drowned out their conversation. By the time it had gone, Sasha had managed to calm down a bit from the bright red colour she'd turned.

"He's dead! He died! The last time I saw him we were floating in the Atlantic with bullets flying around us…and blood…Dead bodies, falling….he….they never found him…."

"Well….if that's him in there, someone must have?"

"No one told me…" Suddenly something dawned on Sasha. She pulled out her mobile from her pocket and scrolled through the numbers.

"Shit."

"What is it?"

"I had Martha's number, at the pub in Tregiffen….Shit." The realization hit her. "This is a new phone!". Of course, her old one, the number that anyone in Tregiffen had, was likely somewhere at the bottom of the sea.

Leigh smiled as an idea dawned.

"Internet – ramp office. Google 'em!" Sasha rushed in, in a fever, forced Mike who had popped in to change his gloves to log in for her.

She searched for the listing for the 'Sailors Rest' and picked up the phone next to her.

Leigh couldn't stand still, hopping around opposite her

like she had ants in her pants. Mike didn't bother asking what was going on…he didn't quite think he wanted to know, so he left them to it and headed back out to his pushback tug.

"Hi can I speak to Martha? Jimmy? Oh… No, it's OK. No I was just… Ned? Is that you? It's Sasha…Oh…what are you doing there? ... Oh no...I...um…."

She glanced up at Leigh, eyes wide. Leigh made a rolling motion with her hand at Sasha, desperate for her to get on with it so she could find out what was going on. Sasha continued, listening and responding to Ned on the other end of the phone.

"Um…yes, today. He's…yes I saw him today…Yes… Ah I wondered why…in the sea, of course...OK…listen give my regards…send my love to everyone…" She hung up the phone and stared at it, sadly.

"Jimmy died."

Leigh raised her eyebrows and waited for more.

"Poor Martha" Sasha sighed. It was almost as though she'd forgotten the point of her call.

"Sasha? " Leigh broke in,"Sorry...I am really sorry, not nice to get news like that, but…."

"They've been trying to call. The only number they had on file for me was….this is a new phone. Old one is at the bottom of the fucking Atlantic."

"And…."

"Oh," Sasha recovered herself and started to fill Leigh in, "Air & Sea rescue never found him….because the bastard had already swam ashore…"

Sasha seemed very angry, wringing her hands, eyes wide and almost shouting. "Bullet hole in his leg and everything. Minack. "

"Huh? "

"Um, up the coast, quiet, beach next to the Minack….pretty much deserted at night – he crawled, hobbled, whatever, for close to 5 hours before anyone drove past to pick him up…."

"But, you were being de-briefed. Didn't they say anything?"

"They said they'd…" Sasha suddenly came to a conclusion. Having turned away from Leigh, she turned back to look her in the eye.

"What I actually heard was "Call off the search and notify his family""

"That's it?" Leigh checked. Sasha nodded.

"They did say SOMETHING about a body but…"

"Not completely conclusive then? They could have said something"

"I guess they thought I'd talk to someone later. "

"You didn't ask?"

"As far as I thought, they'd just confirmed he'd died..."

"He seems very, very, much alive now..." Leigh stopped when she noticed her friend welling up. "Oh god, I'm sorry."

Perched on a handrail as another airplane roared past, they both stared after it dreamily. Sasha sniffed back and composed herself, before heading away from her friend, towards the terminal. She couldn't face him yet, she knew. She had to think. In the meantime, she had the rest of her shift to finish. Preferably filing the flight paperwork for the dispatchers; in the office; out of sight.

Leigh had other ideas. She followed Sasha, knowing they had to go through the arrivals hall as their quickest route back. She raced past Sasha, through the door, scurrying past Kevin in Immigration before he could say anything and straight over to the Customs collective, standing squarely in front of Colan.

This man was nothing like the gruff, rough, scary monster of a man she'd had described to her. He smiled at her sweetly, meltingly gorgeously. Leigh could have sworn a superhero-type sparkle came off his teeth when he grinned. She smiled back.

Oh God this is the right thing to do, she thought to herself, and thrust her hand out.

"Hi! I'm Leigh..." she began.

A hint of recognition came over Col's face when she announced her name. He was about to say something, but she didn't give him the chance.

"I work on check-in. My friend over there has the biggest crush on you." She pointed directly at Sasha, who was bright red again and trying her best to hide behind a very interested Kevin; just as Leigh's handheld radio crackled into life.

"Control to Papa Sierra Leigh – can you and Sasha meet the Jersey on Stand 22?" Mina's authoritative voice shouted through the walkietalkies.

"Copied – Sasha's busy in the baggage but Pilar's here" Leigh announced, and she ran away like a giggling schoolgirl, yanking a shocked and confused Pilar by the hand on the way past and leading her out. Leigh winked at Pilar and whispered, "I'll explain on the way".

Sasha watched them go, horrified. Kevin very quickly caught on to the ethos, if not the details, of what was happening and stepped aside, nonchalantly, so Sasha had nowhere to hide.

Colan started to head in their direction. Sasha closed her eyes, hoping that when she opened them, she'd find this wasn't happening. No such luck. Kevin bowed out and went back to his office, winking at Sasha on his way. Try as she might to hold her composure, inside she was shaking violently, from shock, anticipation and the mere proximity to the man who had made her lose herself so many times.

She managed miraculously to look up at him. His dark hair was immaculately groomed, he was well-shaven and his perfect, muscled frame modelled the smart uniform very, very well. So very, very, different from when they had first met; and yet, still the same effect on her as every other time they'd been this close. Sasha felt as though she were burning up.

Colan, on the other hand, was trying his best to remain composed. Not least for his new charges who were watching from the Customs office with interest; to his Immigration counterpart, Kevin, whom he'd liked when they had met that morning and knew they'd get on very well with. Mainly, he didn't want to frighten, or hurt, this amazing creature he knew he'd scared and hurt so much already.

God, she looks prim and proper in that suit.

Col looked her over. Minimal make-up and no nail polish, he noticed, not over-done like some of the girls could be, but a smartened up, workplace version of his gorgeous, care-free, beach-days, and nights, Sasha.

To be fair, he knew he'd had more time to prepare himself for this reunion than she had, so was prepared, and knew he'd have to take the lead.

He held out his hand and held her stare. "Colan Treharne, HM Customs Service."

"Sasha P..p..pender," she faltered "Ground handling. Treharne?" He winked, his eyes glistening like and excited schoolboy.

"Good to meet you." He extended a hand and surrounded her trembling fingers in an effort to steady her.

"Likewise." Sasha straightened up. Aware she was being watched by others around the baggage hall, she attempted to stay outwardly composed. "As the Customer Services Trainer, I was, uhm, wondering if I could…" She was faltering now, trying to find words.

"Trainer too?" he sounded impressed, as the immigration hall began to fill with another incoming flight, unsuspecting passengers bustling around them intent only on finding their own luggage.

Sasha blushed. "Uhm" she stepped back for a passenger to get by, "I was wondering…"

"I wonder if…" Colan started simultaneously. "Sorry, you go…" he tried to correct himself…

A rowdy group of holidaymakers returning from the sun pushed past Colan, knocking him forward, straight into Sasha.

Pushing her towards the wall, he instinctively braced himself to stop from crushing her, at the same time putting a protective arm around her as though to avoid her injury from hitting the wall behind her.

For seemingly endless moments they held that position. Neither wanting it to end for fear, from experience, that it may never come again.

No one but they seemed to notice, or even care, about their moment. The half-inebriated party-going girls who had just returned from Ibiza were entertaining the crowds queuing with their passports in hand, dressed in combinations of denim hot pants and crop tops; it was barely possible to hear oneself think let alone hold a conversation of the kind Col and Sasha needed.

She caught her breath again and spoke, almost in a whisper, “Would you, as chief Customs officer, happen to have your own, private, office?” trying to avoid his gaze, wishing she could keep hold of the strong, comforting hand that was wrapped around hers.

“Good idea…” he murmured, looking up in the direction of the Customs suite, and trying to look as official as possible strode across the hall.

Sasha followed, exuding fake confidence. Colan smiled genuinely to Olga at her desk in the main customs office.

Almost a part of the furniture in this place, she waved at Sasha. “Hi Olga, just discussing the meet and greet sessions for the new trainees” Sasha smiled, and talked far more quickly than necessary, as though required to explain her presence.

“Met our new hunk then? “ The portly older lady smiled.

“Commanding officer madam!” joked Colan with her, easily as though he’d been there for years, not his first day on the job.

“Pah, I’m everyone’s mum in this place! Coffee, Sash?”

Olga enquired, clicking the switch on her kettle in her own private tea corner.

"Olga, I'll be talking in my office for a …" Colan was cut off by Olga's phone ringing.

"Hang on a sec, boss. Hello, baggage office? Oh hi Leigh; yeah they're just going into his off…..What?" Olga listened intently, and glanced at Sasha and Colan in turn. Sasha blushed and looked down. "I seeee. I'll let you know about that then Leigh. What extension are you on? OK, thanks." Olga grinned at them both and put the phone down. "I'll be holding your calls for a bit then?"

Colan's eyes widened, and in an effort to hide any nerves, turned suddenly and disappeared into the office. Olga winked at the nervous, blushing Sasha as she hurried in behind him.

Colan closed the door behind her. She dared not turn around. Suddenly overcome with the realisation that they were alone, together for the first time since the last night in Sennen Cove, Colan was motionless.

Sasha felt her eyes welling up again, but would not allow weakness to show. Still determined to be strong and not let him back in, she spun to face him. She hadn't expected him to be even better looking than she allowed herself to remember.

"You're dead! What are you DOING here?!" she accused, shaking her head, as though trying to clear it.

"I took a promotion…"

“Promotion?! From being dead?”

“Sideways transfer…” He shrugged, and started talking fast from the nerves “with maybe a step down. Not that they really minded, the operation wasn’t a total success after…I mean, they arrested Juan but we’re not really any closer to shutting the whole thing down”

Colan was really feeling pressure now. Sod Cornish fishermen in storms on rough seas; and smugglers; and the emotional rollercoaster he’d gone through in Cornwall trying to suppress the things he felt for her and then trying to protect her.

“The body. They were talking. They said they found a body?” Sasha, still flustered, remembered back to the overheard snippets in the debrief with Martin King. Col paused for a moment, and then realisation hit him. “They found two of the dead men. Pulled them out of the sea.”

This honesty, this real-life moment, unscripted, was something he was really unfamiliar with

“God, Sasha, I didn’t know….how to approach you, find you…I mean, I knew where you were, but...”

“So you think working here every day is a good way to rub my nose in it?” she flustered.

“I love you”

“After everything, you made me…” she pretended not to hear him, and faltered, trying to find the word to describe how she’d been feeling

"I love you. "

"Hurt" She cried "I lost you, I grieved, I cried. " Sasha let the tears flow again.

What the hell, she thought, he's seen me cry before, and he walked away. Colan fell forward and grabbed her.

"Sash, I love you. The morning you walked down to that quayside, you ruined me"

She couldn't look at him, she was far too emotional, but the feeling of being in his strong, steady arms again was creating a feeling of awakening.

It was beginning not to matter where she was, when they were, what was going on around them or whether the next step was facing rabid gun-toting pirates, or her nosey, gossip mongering colleagues – all that mattered was that if she raised her head and opened her eyes now, right at this moment…

Colan was scared to death. She was shaking, physically shaking, hard. Is she cold? Is she crying? The lump in his throat was almost enough to stop him breathing.

He wrapped his arms around her and held her as close as he could without hurting her – God forbid if he was hurting her again…

Sasha opened her eyes and couldn't believe her luck. She was still looking into his. She was still in his arms. She couldn't hear anything but crashing waves but she saw his mouth moving, "Sasha…I love you!"

25

She stopped shaking. Her tears had stopped too. She was almost smiling…

“Sasha, say something” he begged. She took a moment to gather herself; catch her breath. She raised her eyes and stared up into his questioning gaze.

“When the hell are you going to kiss me? Please?” was all she could just about push out before she felt like exploding from the need his closeness was creating in her.

He heaved a sigh of relief, grinned and claimed her mouth with his own.

God this is good, Sasha thought as his kisses moved down her neck again, but not good enough. She felt for his tie and removed it as quickly as she could, tossing it across the room.

Colan was stopped in his tracks and looked into her face …. “Really? “

“Lock the bloody door will you? “ Sasha ordered

fiercely. Colan smiled at her mischievously.

“On my first day?”

“Trust me,“ Sasha said “You’ve been talked about far too much around here already for anyone to be surprised…”

“What?!” Colan choked, surprised but still roaming his hands all over her behind, before moving to fiddle with the buttons of her immaculate blazer.

“Seriously? After what you’ve done to me and turned me into?”

Colan smiled and raised an interested eyebrow “And that is?”

“At the moment a quivering fucking mess if you don’t do something about it – but we have some serious talking to do after.” Col stopped.

“I should take some responsibility then…”

Sasha couldn’t believe he had stopped. She looked at him quizzically. He slowly undid his top few buttons, taking control of the situation and slowing down, as if to tease her, and she dared to hope he’d continue. He stopped undoing his buttons and moved away from her suddenly.

“Hot in here isn’t it?” he muttered.

“If you say so” she answered, unsure where this was going.

"I wasn't going to try this, not yet, to avoid you sullying your reputation, but if everyone who counts is likely to understand anyway…" he fished around in the pocket of the wax overcoat – the same from Tregiffen, she smiled at the memory of him wearing it.

Sasha's smile suddenly dropped when Colan pulled out what was very obviously a box from a jewelry store.

"Please…tell me that's a pair of ear-rings?" She gasped.

"That depends….if it's not, would your answer be yes?" Col tried his best to keep his expression sincere; as opposed to nervous as hell, scared to death she would laugh in his face.

"God, this is a dream? Or a joke?" Sasha paused. From the look on his face he was serious. And every fibre of her being wanted him; wanted to be with him for the rest of her life; but could she really do this so suddenly?

"Sasha," Col approached her, and got down on one knee, "I love you. You've changed my life, more than I thought could be possible. I want you to be there for the rest of it….Marry me, Sasha."

Initially stunned, speechless, she finally found some words to string a sentence together.

"I know nothing about you!"

Which was hardly true, she told herself, she just wasn't sure which version of him she knew best.

"So we call a long engagement. I want you to know

everything. And today's my birthday. My REAL birthday." He stood in front of her and pulled her to him again.

He bent slowly and kissed her, deeply, slowly, more passionately than anything they had done before. She spoke into his mouth in between kisses.

"I think I know enough" She reached for his belt buckle, "I can get the details later. I might even let you stay at my place on the first date…"

Col groaned

"Can I take that as a yes and we get on with this?" He pushed her blazer off and unbuttoned her blouse before she knew what was happening, "Yes plea…OH" She gasped as his trousers dropped to the floor, he lifted her deftly onto his desk , her skirt rising higher and his head bowing towards her breasts, pulling them out of her bra, seemingly all in one move.

Col's hand moved up her thigh as he took her right nipple in his mouth. He groaned,

"Do they make you wear tights with your uniform?"

"I might invest in a suspender belt" She giggled. She wriggled out of her tights and underwear at the same time.

"Oh! About bloody time!" Sasha moaned as Col slid one hand between her legs, and with his other, guided her own hand to his erection. Col lifted his head and looked into her eyes

“I never dreamed my first day was going to…” He stopped everything for a moment “… be like this”.

“Does that mean you don’t have any…? ” Sasha began

“Protection?” he continued for her; simultaneously producing a small packet from pocket on his satchel which lay on the desk next to them.

“Sorry,” Sasha whispered, “I know we’re…”she paused, to savour the word for a moment, “engaged, now, but… Oh God hurry up…Please!”

Colan smiled at her – genuine, loving, caring, open, honest smile, like a best friend and partner in crime all in one.

He entered her tantalisingly slowly; so different from the fever that had been consuming them for the past half an hour. Sasha gasped at the pleasure of having him inside her once again. This feels so right, every time it happens, she thought to herself.

Without dropping each other’s gaze, they moved together in rhythm until the Sasha could feel the explosion inside her reaching the surface. Knowing full well there were probably more people in the outer office than there had been on their way in, she dropped her face and buried her mouth into his shoulder to muffle her moan. Col held her tighter as she shuddered around him and reveled in the joy of her orgasm, pushed him over the edge himself. He came as another aircraft thundered by the small window out onto the apron, thankfully drowning out his own groan. They slumped to the floor and leaned against the desk, Sasha's head on Col's heaving chest; enjoying the comfort, closeness and joy of the moment.

"You do realise, that door is being watched intensely from the outside?" Sasha stated.

"Of course" Col smiled down at her. "How long do you think we could safely stay in here without being discovered?"

"*Someone* distracted me so much I've lost track of time!" Sasha ran a hand across Col's chest and sighed in admiration.

"Well that really helps the situation, thanks" he laughed at her. He got up and held out a hand to help her up.

Dusting themselves off and regaining somewhere near presentable uniforms, Sasha turned to him, kissed him once again, passionately but quickly, and muttered "Happy Birthday"

Col took a deep breath and opened the door. Amazingly, they found only Olga, seemingly deeply engrossed in her daily reports; and Leigh, sat next to the coffee corner patiently. Both women looked up expectantly as soon as the pair came out.

"Honestly, those planes rattle past this office at the most inopportune moments, don't they, Olga?" suggested Leigh with a grin plastered from ear to ear. She took one look at Sasha's shy but telling grin and ran over to hug Colan, surprising him greatly.

"Sorry," she said, almost insincerely "I just had to cop a feel before you're officially taken!"

Leigh's radio crackled into life, "Control, Leigh and Sasha – CDG's late; can you stay?" Leigh looked at Sasha; Sasha looked at Colan. Her heart sank. Bloody Paris Charles De Gaulle and their Air Traffic Control strikes. Today of all days she wanted her shift to finish on time.

"Hey I'm going to be here 'till that clears anyway." He reminded her. Sasha smiled and called Mina back to let her know they were fine to wait.

There was an awkward silence while the four all swapped glances.

Col decided to break the silence and gestured to Sasha.

"Better, um…do this?" He held his hand up, holding the ring box, gesturing it towards her. She blushed and caught it deftly when he threw.

"Bugger that" shouted Olga "You put it on her yourself!"

Leigh was overwhelmed with surprise.

"You fucking proposed?! In work?! How bloody unromantic is that? Sash, you made out he was like some romantic novel hero."

As Colan reached for Sasha's hand to place the ring on her finger, she stared deeply into the eyes she knew were hers to stare into for the rest of her life, and told her best friend, "Oh it was romantic."

Colan pulled her forward and kissed her, proving to Leigh and Olga that he was far more than a mere romantic hero; as even those watching went weak at the knees.

"I think I should probably call my therapist" whispered Sasha.

Olga clasped her hands in delight and Leigh let out a squeal.

"I bloody love working here!"

Landing Lights is a series of tales linked by a place – a regional airport in the UK. The characters who work there and their lives are intertwined and yet individual; romantic; adventurous; tragic; ultimately giving a place, a series of tin sheds and boarding gates, a life of its own, a living, breathing, ever changing, community. Look out for "Airborne", the next novel in the Landing Lights series, and follow Leigh's career as she takes off...

About the Author

R.A.Watson-Wood lives in Wales but has lived a varied life since being born in Cornwall to Scottish and Welsh parents, from growing up at sea on cargo ships, to living in pubs, to traveling the USA and Brazil alone, to working in Travel and Aviation for many years. Writing since a very young age, Dreamboat is the first in a series of fictional tales set around a regional airport and its' workers.

Manufactured by Amazon.ca
Bolton, ON